There's no message, just a photo. Or rather a scan. A scan of part of a page of my diary. I think for a minute that I'm going to be sick and then I feel like I'm being watched. I actually look around the room for a second, as if I'm expecting someone to jump out, laughing.

For Mum and Dad

I thought writing the acknowledgements would be the easy bit, but no...

Massive thanks to my agent Alice Williams, my editor Catherine Coe, and the team at Orchard, for believing in me and Della.

I honestly couldn't have written this (or any) book without my amazing WriteWords and We Should Be Writing friends, especially Claire, Debs, Emily, Fionnuala, Sarah and Zoe. An extra-special mention goes to Luisa Plaja for keeping me motivated, sane and entertained and for doing such a fabulous job with Chicklish.

Thanks also to my sister Leanne for throwing the party at which my diary went missing, giving me the idea for the book; to Diane Shipley for the Hannibal suggestion and book trolley lunches; and to my in-laws, Enid and Andrew, for all the babysitting, cooking, washing and gardening.

Most of all, thank you to David, Harry and Joe for making me laugh every single day.

ORCHARD BOOKS
338 Euston Road, London NW1 3BH
Orchard Books Australia
Level 17/207 Kent Street, Sydney, NSW 2000

First published in 2010 by Orchard Books

A Paperback Original

ISBN 978 1 40830 427 3

Text © Keris Stainton 2010

The right of Keris Stainton to be identified as the author of this work has been asserted by her in accordance with the Copyright, Designs and Patents Act, 1988.

A CIP catalogue record for this book is available from the British Library.

1 3 5 7 9 10 8 6 4 2

Printed in Great Britain

Orchard Books is a division of Hachette Children's Books, an Hachette UK company.

www.hachette.co.uk

Della says: OMG!

Keris Stainton

ORCHARD BOOKS

"Is that what you're wearing?" Maddy asks me.

I look down – jeans, boots, a white vest, a red shirt unbuttoned. "Yeah. Why?"

"It's not very..." She screws her face up. "Sexy?"

"Sexy?" I look down again. I can see down the vest to my non-existent boobs. "I wasn't trying to be sexy."

"And it shows." Maddy opens my wardrobe and starts flicking through the clothes; it doesn't take long, I've never been that interested in fashion.

"God, Del," Maddy turns to look at me. "Is this everything?"

"Yeah. Well, apart from tops and stuff in the drawers."

"What about Jamie? Has she got anything?"

"She will have, but she won't lend it to me."

"She might if I ask her and tell her what we need it for."

"What do we need it for?" I ask, but she's already left for my sister Jamie's room. I get on OK with my sister, but we mostly avoid each other. If she's not out with her boyfriend, Jack, she's in her room listening to music. And I wouldn't dream of borrowing anything of hers without asking. Not again, anyway. Mads once talked me into taking one of Jamie's bags on a night out, and when Jamie found out she went berserk and smacked me round the head with it.

"Ta-da!" Maddy says, bursting through the door holding a black and white minidress, black leggings, silver shoes and the very same silver bag I last saw bouncing onto the floor off my head.

"How did you—"

"It's all about the charm, baby," she says, laying the clothes out on my bed. "And she agreed that you'd never pull Dan Bailey dressed like that!"

"Dan?" I whisper. I can feel my face heating up.

"Didn't I tell you he's coming?" Maddy says brightly, as she starts tugging my shirt off me.

"You know you didn't," I say. I pull the shirt off and throw it back into the bottom of my wardrobe, then pull the vest over my head and drop it on the floor.

"You should take better care of your clothes," Maddy says. She glances down at my chest. "Have you got a Wonderbra?"

"You know I haven't."

Sighing, Maddy heads back to my sister's room.

Dan Bailey. I have loved Dan Bailey since the first time I saw him. My first day of primary school. Sitting on the floor in Mrs Robinson's class. The mums were all sitting at the back of the room and my mum had promised me she wouldn't leave without saying goodbye, but when I turned to check she was still there, she'd gone. I cried, obviously, and Dan – he was Daniel then – came up and gave me a box of crayons.

I was stunned. Not just because he'd come to cheer me up. Not just because he was easily the cutest boy in the class (yes, you notice even at that

7

age) but because the crayons were brand new, unopened. Jamie is only two years older than me and up until then I'd only ever had her hand–me–downs, which she usually managed to completely wreck before they got to me.

"Can I open them?" I'd breathed.

Daniel shrugged and went back to the sand pit. Mrs Robinson kissed the top of my head and said, "Of course!"

That – eleven years ago – was the longest conversation I've ever had with Dan Bailey.

"Here you go," Maddy says, brandishing Jamie's white Wonderbra at me. I take it from her and turn towards the wardrobe to change bras. I've never been comfortable with getting my clothes off in front of anyone else. Maddy will just strip off and get changed in front of me and I don't know where to look, but I prefer a bit of privacy.

"I can still see your boobs in the mirror, you know," Maddy says.

"You shouldn't be looking!" I say as I hook the bra at the back.

"I'm not," Maddy says. "I'm just saying I could if I wanted to."

I roll my eyes and pull Jamie's dress over my head. I have to admit, it looks quite good. Between the dress and the bra I almost look like I've got boobs and it gives me a bit of a waist, too.

"It suits you," Maddy says. "I knew it would!"

I pull the leggings on and then the shoes. They kill. "I can't wear these all night!"

"Of course you can."

"They really hurt!"

"Don't worry, your feet'll go numb in a couple of hours."

"Oh, well, that's something to look forward to."

Maddy starts dragging a brush through my long, brown hair. "What are you going to do with it?" she asks.

"Ponytail?"

"Nah, boys like long hair. Leave it down."

I shake my head. "No, it drives me mad—"

"God, just leave it down! It looks good. Why do you always have to argue?"

"Why do you always have to be so bossy?"

"Because I know what's best for you."

And because she's got three little sisters and she treats me like a fourth.

"And what's that?"

"Getting dolled up, going to your party and getting off with Dan Bailey."

I snort. "Yeah, right. And it's not my party, it's Jamie's." Next week, my sister is going away to work for the summer, before going to university in London, in September. This party is her big send-off. "And how do you even know he's going to come?"

"Sid told me." Sid has been Maddy's boyfriend since the last year of primary school. Seriously.

"And how does Sid know?"

"He asked Dan."

"What?"

She speaks slowly as if I'm an idiot. "Sid asked Dan if he was coming to your party. Dan said yes."

I can feel my cheeks getting hot again. "Why did he ask him?"

"To see if he was coming. God!"

"No. I mean, were they talking, or what? Or did Sid just go up to him and ask him?"

"I don't know, I think he saw him at football or something and he asked him."

"But why? I mean, did he say something about me?"

"You're so self-obsessed," she says, joking (I hope). "No, I doubt he said anything about you."

"So what makes you think tonight will be any different from any other night? What makes you think that Dan Bailey will even notice I'm alive?"

"Because you're wearing a Wonderbra, a dress, silver shoes, make-up—"

"Oh no."

"Oh yes."

"I'm not wearing make-up."

Maddy turns and empties her make-up bag out onto my bed. "Sit down."

I sit.

"You look lovely," my mum says. "Steven, Steven! Come and have a look at Della."

This is why I hate to get done up. I hate being the centre of attention. I'd much rather look like myself and let everyone ignore me.

"A pretty girl..." my dad sings, as he comes through the double doors into the lounge, "...is like a melody!"

Maddy snorts and my dad grabs her hands and swings her round, singing 'Brown Eyed Girl', the way he always does. I wouldn't mind, but her eyes are hazel.

"It's all my stuff," Jamie says, coming down the stairs. She's wearing the shortest boy shorts with a skimpy vest and she's got a face mask on.

"Jesus," my dad says. "Go and get dressed, will you? You'll frighten the cat."

Jamie sticks her tongue out at him and sashays (I'm sorry, but there's no other word for it) into the kitchen. I see my parents exchange a look and Maddy elbows me.

"So, when are you going?" I ask.

"Oh, that's charming, that is," Dad says. "Can't wait to get rid of us!"

"No, I—"

"Maybe we won't go," Mum says. "Maybe we'll stay and party with you girls. It's not every day one of our babies goes off to make her way in the world."

Dad does some hip-swivelling, I cover my face with my hands and, from the kitchen, I hear Jamie say, "Oh, for God's sake."

"We'll be out of your hair in no time," Dad says, still dancing. "As long as we have your solemn promise that there'll be no boys and no drinking."

"No way," Maddy says. "It's all girls. Jelly and ice cream, a children's entertainer and then we're going to do each other's hair and watch Disney films."

"That's what I like to hear!" He wanders through to the kitchen, calling, "Say no to drugs," over his shoulder.

"I love your dad," Maddy says, as she always does.

"You do look lovely," my mum says. She reaches up and hooks my hair behind one ear. "You should wear your hair down more often."

"Dan Bailey's coming," Jamie says, as she heads back upstairs, carrying a pack of celery, a jar of mayonnaise and a jar of peanut butter.

"Are you pregnant?" Mum says, nodding at the food.

"Yeah, right," Jamie says. "You use more calories eating celery than there are actually in celery so then you've got calories to spare." She waves the peanut butter at us, as if that explains it. "And I'm lining my stomach. For the jelly and ice cream."

"Come on, we'd better get going," Dad says, coming back in with his jacket on and shrugging Mum's coat over her shoulders.

"Have a lovely time," Mum says. She reaches out and hugs us both.

"We will, thanks."

"Good luck with Dan."

"Thanks."

Maddy and I back out of the room and then sit on the stairs until they leave.

"Maybe we should've let them stay," Maddy says, ridiculously, once we're sure they've gone. (I wouldn't put it past them to hide in the garden and sneak back in when we weren't expecting it.)

"No way," I say. "Dan would end up getting off with my mum!"

Mum used to be a model. When we were little, she was away working quite a lot and Dad stayed home with us. But then they started their own business and she began coming to pick us up from school in leather trousers, boots, silky tops. Everyone wondered why their dads had started coming to collect them when they'd never bothered before. She's still beautiful now, but I don't think she can quite believe she's a housewife in Lancashire (albeit one who owns a chain of delis) and not, I don't know, married to Rod Stewart or Simon le Bon or someone.

I can't quite believe it myself. Even now she looks out of place at parents' evenings or whatever. It's not just that she's so gorgeous, it's the way she holds herself, like she knows everyone's looking at her. Once we were walking down the street and someone shouted her name. She turned, flicking her hair almost in slow motion like she was on a red carpet or something – and it was only the postman. She didn't look disappointed though, she looked as pleased to see him as if he'd been George Clooney.

The thing about having a beautiful mother and being, well, ordinary yourself, is that everyone is so shocked when they see her. If I had a pound for every time someone said, "Is that your mum?!" in this incredulous, amazed way, I'd be super-rich. And then I see them look at me and then at her and back at me as if they're wondering what happened. And they may as well, because my dad's pretty gorgeous too, which is why Maddy loves him so much (and he's funny, which helps).

And Jamie's the same (as mum, I mean). She's got that X factor. Boys are always falling in love with her and doing dramatic things to get her attention. No one's ever done anything dramatic to get my attention. In fact, when I've given boys my attention, they haven't even noticed.

"So what are you going to say to Dan?" Maddy asks later, as we started locking 'breakables' away in cupboards.

"Me? Why me?"

"Why not you?"

I blink at her.

"Listen, what does Dr Phil say?" Maddy loves Dr Phil, the psychologist guy she's always watching on Living or somewhere. "If you always do what you've always done, you'll always get what you've always got."

"Pardon?"

"It's the definition of insanity."

"I thought that was talking to yourself."

"No, that's the first sign of madness. Anyway, what have you always done, where Dan's concerned?"

"Um. Nothing?"

"Exactly. And where's that got you?"

"Nowhere."

"So what do you need to do?"

"I don't know."

"Something! And that will get you somewhere!"

"And they gave him his own show for that?"

"No, he was Oprah Winfrey's lawyer or something. But listen, it makes sense."

"But the other thing doing nothing has got me is not being embarrassed and humiliated. But doing something might."

"Feel the fear and do it anyway!"

"I don't want to."

"Hard luck."

We've just about got all the breakables locked

away – and Jamie has just come downstairs looking, horrifyingly (for me, not for her), pretty much exactly like our mother – when people start to arrive. First our friends Rosy and Amber and then a load of my sister's friends, who are really loud and already pretty drunk.

Two guys immediately set up record decks – who brings their own decks to a party? – and the girls slump on the sofas and watch them put records on and take records off. I'd brought my iPod and docking station down, but I decide there and then to lock them away, too.

As I head up to my room, there's already a couple – I don't know them – snogging on the stairs.

"They didn't waste much time," Maddy says, elbowing me. When I come back down, we go into the kitchen and Maddy gets us both cans of Red Bull.

"Hey!" Sid says, coming up behind us. He puts an arm around each of our shoulders. Maddy kisses him and says hello to his friend Leo, who's never very far away from Sid. Maddy sometimes jokes that it's like she's got two boyfriends, because she hardly ever sees Sid without Leo (except when they, you know, REALLY need to be alone). She doesn't mind though, because Leo is gorgeous and funny and they get on brilliantly. I think he's secretly in love with Maddy, but she says it's more likely that he's secretly in love with Sid.

"Want some of this?" Sid says. He waves a miniature of vodka towards Maddy's Red Bull. He pours some in both of our cans and then says, "So are you up for it?"

"What?" I ask.

"A party!"

Oh. "Umm. Yeah, kind of," I say.

"That's the spirit," he says, laughing. "You're looking gorgeous, by the way, Della."

"Oi!" Maddy shoves him. "She's got a plan tonight."

"Oh yeah," Sid says, grinning. "Dan Bailey."

"Shhhhh!"

"Is he here?" Maddy asks.

"I've not seen him," Sid admits. "But I think there's someone shagging in the lav. Could be him."

"Shut up," Maddy says. "Tonight's the night for Della and Dan."

"Sounds like a dodgy porno."

"And you'd know," Maddy says.

We follow Sid and Leo into the front room. The music is deafening, but there are only about eight people in the room: a couple, Lauren and Connor, who we know from school, and a bunch of lads who've obviously got bored with the records and are now sifting through Dad's CDs. There's a guy with blue hair and headphones playing on a PSP and a girl with dyed black hair texting. Wow. Some party.

"Par-tay!" Sid says and shoves me and Maddy back out into the hall. We all go back through the kitchen and out of the back door. There are more people in the garden than the house and the music is still loud enough that a couple of Jamie's (male) friends are pogoing on the patio. We sit down on a bench under the back window and Sid lights a cigarette and hands it to Maddy.

"I thought you'd given up?" I say.

"I have," Maddy says. "I'm a social smoker and this is a social occasion."

I roll my eyes as Maddy passes the cig on to Leo.

The back door opens again and a crowd of about twelve spills out, boys and girls who already seem drunk. I suck my stomach in and try to arrange my face into a casual expression in case Dan is with them. But he isn't. One of the lads trips off the patio and falls face-down on the lawn, while the rest of them cackle and whoop.

I get up and go back into the house, wondering where my sister might be. Just as I walk into the hall, I see Dan coming out of the lounge. I feel myself starting to blush. I turn to go back outside, but I hear him speak.

"What?" I turn around again. "Sorry, did you say something?" My voice is tiny.

He grins; he's got the most gorgeous grin. "Yeah. I said, what's going on out there?" He nods towards the garden. "Fighting already?"

"No, no." I walk backwards into the kitchen until I hit the table and then I stop. He follows me in and stops in front of me. "Someone fell over," I say, brilliantly. I reach behind me to steady myself and knock over a bottle of beer.

"Shit!" I grab a tea towel off the side and mop it up. It's dripping onto the floor. I bend down and dab at the floor, and then, as I get up, bang my head on the table. "Shit!"

Dan laughs. "Are you OK?"

"Yeah," I say without getting up. I think about actually crawling under the table and just staying there, but Dan says, "Are you getting up?"

"Yeah." I scramble to my feet. I don't think I've ever blushed so hard.

"You look like you could do with some fresh air," Dan says, opening the back door. I follow him out and see Maddy's eyebrows shoot up behind her fringe. She lolls her tongue out of her mouth and I pull a face at her.

The boys all greet Dan with hoots and thumps, the way boys do. I'm edging back towards Maddy when Dan turns to me. "Have you got a drink?" he says.

I nod.

"Do you want to sit down?" He gestures at a bench at the side of the garden, in front of the shed.

"Yeah, thanks." I sit down, thinking he's still

worried about my head, but then he surprises me by sitting down next to me.

"Nice house," he says.

I look around like an idiot, as if I'm not sure whose house it is. "Thanks."

"Your mum was a model, right?" he asks. I feel myself start to blush. Yeah, stupid me, thinking he was interested in me when he just wants to know about my mum. You'd think I'd learn, but I never do.

"She was, yeah," I say. "In the eighties."

"Cool."

We both just sit there and then Dan says, "I like a lot of eighties music."

"Yeah?" I ask. I wouldn't have thought he'd be into all that cheesy eighties stuff at all. "Like what?"

"I like Madness, Simple Minds, The Cure."

"Oh, right," I say, smiling. "I thought you meant the cheesy stuff. Like Kajagoogoo. You know the *Now That's What I Call Music* CDs?"

He nods.

"Well, my mum and dad have got loads of them from, like, number five or something. They're on cassette and every now and then they get them out and dance around to these ridiculous songs like 'The Safety Dance'."

"Men Without Hats," Dan says, and I laugh.

"Yes! Or 'Kayleigh' by Marillion."

"I like that one!" Dan says, pretending to be offended.

I smile at him and he smiles back until I start to get embarrassed and have to look away. I try to think of more songs – I should know loads, I've heard those albums often enough – but I can't think of any. And anyway, I'm worried that the moment's gone and if I just sit here naming eighties bands he'll think I'm a complete dork.

"They have eighties nights at the Cav," Dan says. "Do you fancy going some time?"

I glance at him, but he's looking straight ahead, down the garden. The Cav is this under-18s club in town. Did he really just ask me to go there with him? I don't know what to say. I mean, what if he's asking me for a bet or something? What if I say yes, and he bursts out laughing and runs over to his mates? I'd die. Literally. I would quite literally die. Here, by the shed.

But then I don't get a chance to say anything at all, because Kyle Armstrong comes flying through the door and knocks Dan off the bench and onto the grass, shouting "All pile on!"

Boys start running from every corner of the garden and, as I pass the pile, I see Dan at the bottom. His face is bright red, but he's laughing.

In the kitchen, I pick up another Red Bull and wander into the hall – which is crammed – where Sid grabs me and tops it up with vodka. I try the front room, which is a bit more lively, but still more a games room than anything else (and it already smells of farts). I get to the front door and actually think about leaving, but I know Maddy would go berserk if I did.

Anyway, this is my house – where would I go? Usually, I'd go to Maddy's, but she's in my garden. God, I hate parties! What are you supposed to do? I don't know what to do with myself. I lean back against the door and try to look casual. I want to look like 'I'm so relaxed here alone, checking it all out', rather than 'I've got no friends and I want to go to bed'. I obviously don't pull it off because Jack, Jamie's boyfriend, puts his face really close to mine and says, "Are you OK?"

I lean back a bit. He's definitely a bit too close and his breath smells of – well, I'm not sure what – but it's really strong. Maybe whisky. Or vodka. Or is that the one that doesn't smell?

"Yeah," I start to say. "I'm fi—" I don't get to finish the sentence because Jack's tongue is in my mouth! I push him away. "What do you think you're doing?"

"Oh, come on," he says, but his eyes look unsure. "It's a party!"

"Yeah," I say. "It's Jamie's party. Jamie? Your girlfriend?"

"You're as fucking bad as her," he says and walks off.

I take a couple of steps back and sit down on the stairs. I'm actually shaking. How horrible. I've always thought he was OK, but that was just... horrible. I stare at the streetlights through the glass in the front door. Yellow and fuzzy. I let my eyes unfocus and the lights bounce around like baby chicks. I think about going to bed. Alone. My bedroom door has a lock on it. I could just lock myself in, put a pillow over my head and forget all about this pathetic party.

"What are you doing?" I hear Maddy say and I lift my head up from my knees. "You were talking to Dan, I saw you! What are you doing back in here, on your own?"

I don't want to tell her about Jack because I know she'd go and tell Sid and there'd be a big scene and Jamie would kill me for ruining her party, so instead I say, "He asked me out...I think."

"Dan?" She grins and sits down next to me. "Oh my God! So what did you say?"

"I didn't get a chance to say anything. Kyle Armstrong came out and—"

"All pile on? He is such a knob."

I nod.

"So what are you going to do? Are you waiting for him?"

"I don't know," I say. "What if he was joking? Or it was, like, for a bet or something?"

Maddy rolls her eyes. "You're unbelievable. Of course he wasn't joking. What did he actually say?"

"See!" I say. "You're not convinced either."

"Just tell me what he said."

I tell her and she says, "For God's sake! Get back out in that garden and tell him you'd love to go out with him."

"But what if—"

"Della, you've liked him for years and he's just asked you out. What are you going to do? Say yes, or go upstairs and write all about it in your diary?"

She knows me too well. I stand up and she smacks my bum and says, "Attagirl." She needs to lay off the Red Bull.

I take a deep breath and push the back door open. Kyle Armstrong is lying on his back trying to balance a can on his forehead, while his mates cheer him on. There's no sign of Dan.

I turn to go back into the house, but Gemima Lee is heading out into the garden. God, as if things weren't bad enough. Gemima is the most popular girl at school – with the boys, at least. She's also Dan's best friend. And she hates me. Of course.

"Oh God," she says as soon as she sees me. "Who let you in?"

I can't think of a funny comeback (of course I can't), but I do manage to say, "This is my house, idiot", but as I try to push past her to go back inside, she puts her arm across to stop me. Now, if there's one thing I really hate it's being trapped. When I was little, my sister used to sit on me to stop me doing whatever it was I wanted to do. I hated it then and I hate it now. And I hate it even more because Gemima is doing it to me.

"Just get out of my way, Gemima," I try. I'd hoped to sound menacing, but I actually sound pretty squeaky.

Gemima confirms this by repeating it in a squeaky voice. Great. "I just wondered why you were going inside," she says. "Looking for Dan?"

Crap. Maddy and I have suspected for a while that Gemima knows how I feel about Dan, but we didn't know for sure.

"What makes you think he'd be interested in you?" Gemima says. "I mean, your sister maybe, your mum even, but you?" She throws her head back and laughs, giving me a close-up view of the lovebite on her collarbone. Lovely.

"I just want to go inside, Gemima," I say.

"He knows you like him," Gemima says and I freeze. "He thinks it's very funny."

I feel like I'm going to be sick. In fact, I kind of hope I am. Throwing up on Gemima Lee would be an excellent end to a shitty evening. I yank the door so hard that it hits her in the back and she jerks her arm away, saying, "Jesus! Touchy!" and then laughs again.

I stomp into the house and for a minute I can't even think what I'm supposed to be doing. I realise I'm going to bed, and I'm flooded with relief. No more slobbery boys or bitchy girls or vodka and Red Bull. No more Dan Bailey asking me out as some kind of fucking joke. I climb over the numerous couples practically humping each other on the stairs and I'm almost at my bedroom door when Jack steps in front of me.

I feel like crying, quite honestly. It's like one of those nightmares where you need to be somewhere and you just can't get there because things keep getting in your way and you're getting more and more panicky.

Jack grabs me around the waist and pulls me against him. He smells of Fahrenheit aftershave, which I used to like, but not any more. I feel his slobbery mouth on my neck and I wonder for a second if he's who Gemima got her lovebite from. I try to push him away, but he's holding me really tightly. He pushes me back against the wall and that's when I start to feel a bit scared. As he moves to, I think, kiss me again, I say 'No!' really loudly and try to push him again. He staggers backwards and at first I think I must have got superhuman strength from somewhere, but then I realise Dan is there. Dan had pulled Jack away from me.

I practically fall into my bedroom. I don't know what happens between Dan and Jack, but I do hear someone stumbling down the stairs. I know it must have been Jack when there's a quiet knock on my door frame and Dan pokes his head in. "Are you OK?"

I nod, even though I'm crying, so he must know I'm not.

"Can I come in?" he asks.

I nod again.

He steps just inside the room and says, "Don't let him upset you. He's an arsehole."

"He's my sister's boyfriend."

"He's still an arsehole."

"Don't worry," I say. "I'm OK." I wave my hand as if to say he can go, but he says, "You didn't answer my question. About the Cav?"

"You weren't joking?" I ask.

"Why would I be joking?" he says.

"Gemima Lee said..." I stop myself because I'm aware of how pathetic I sound.

He laughs. "You don't want to listen to what Gemima says. She loves winding people up."

He sits down on the bed next to me. I sigh. I do. I can't help it. I think about Maddy's Dr Phil pep talk and I think about the fact that Dan Bailey has asked me out, twice, and I still haven't said yes and then I just think, well, what do I have to lose?

And I kiss him.

2

When I wake up, I can't quite work out why I'm still dressed. And then I remember – the party! And Dan Bailey! In my room!

I sit up and look around. For a second I had a horrible thought that he might still be here. Not that that would be horrible, exactly. Well, I mean, it wouldn't be horrible at all. But Mum and Dad *finding* him here, that would be horrible. Or horribly embarrassing, anyway. Jamie's had Jack in her room loads of times (and no one's been in any doubt about what they were doing), but certainly not all night.

Oh God. Jack! Jack kissed me, and tried to do who-knows-what. And I have to tell Jamie about it just before she leaves for the summer. Yeah, she's really going to love that. But I don't want to think about Jack.

I want to think about Dan.

Kissing Dan. I kissed Dan. I kissed Dan Bailey.

I stretch my legs to the bottom of the bed and think about last night. And how amazing it was...

We didn't just kiss – we talked too – but the kissing was the most important thing. Especially because it was my first kiss. Well, the first kiss that I actually wanted, that I was actually involved in! (I could think about the fact that my first actual kiss was with Jack. But that's too disgusting, so I'm not going to think about that. I'm going to ignore it. It doesn't count.)

Kissing Dan was amazing. All the times I've spent thinking about kissing and what it would be like, and where our noses would go, or whether he'd stick his tongue in my mouth ('he' not necessarily being Dan Bailey, but any boy I might feasibly end up kissing), and it wasn't like that at all.

His lips were soft. He was holding my hand. I didn't really think or worry while it was happening; I was just doing it, and it felt natural. I still can't believe that it felt natural to be kissing Dan Bailey, sitting on my bed!

I realise that my lips feel a bit sore. He had a little bit of stubble and it rubbed underneath my bottom lip. I touch it with my fingers and smile to myself.

I've got to write about this in my diary.

I clamber out of bed and reach between the mattress and the bed base. I never used to hide my diary, but I suspected for a while that Jamie was reading it (I could practically hear her snorts of laughter every time I opened it) so I started hiding it.

I don't always hide it in the same place, but I'm sure I put it under the mattress yesterday... But I can't find it now. I feel all around in case it got shifted when me and Dan were on the bed...

Just thinking about me and Dan on the bed makes me smile again. I lean back on my heels and try and remember if I did hide the diary there or somewhere else.

I check under the bed. Then under my dressing table. I try the top of the wardrobe and behind the books on my bookcase. Nothing. I even try the gap under the bottom drawer of my chest of drawers, even though I know it's not there; it's a pain in the arse getting the drawer out and I would've remembered.

I must admit, I'm starting to panic a bit. I'm just dragging the mattress off the bed when there's a knock at the door and my mum comes in.

"You OK?" she says, smiling. She notices the state of the bed. "What you doing?"

"I'm just turning the mattress. It felt a bit lumpy."

"Well, it might be an idea to take the bedding off first," she says. She wanders across the room, draws my curtains and then opens the window. She does this whenever she comes into my room; she's got a thing about fresh air. Even if it's snowing outside, Mum'll have all the windows open.

"I just came to tell you that your dad's making a special leaving brunch for Jamie. Can you come down?"

"Yeah," I say, as I yank the sheet off the mattress

and throw it towards my laundry basket. "I'll be five minutes."

"Now would be better," Mum says, picking the sheet off the floor and putting it in the laundry basket. "Your sister's going away for the whole summer, and your dad's been slaving over a hot stove, yadda yadda." She grins.

"OK, OK!" I say and follow her down the stairs.

Dad's outdone himself. He's made, according to him, a Californian breakfast: pancakes, maple syrup, fruit, bacon, home fries, sausages and fried eggs.

"Eggs over easy!" he says proudly.

"This looks amazing!" I say, sitting down.

Jamie wanders in, looking distracted, but grins when she sees the spread on the table.

"Ta-da!" says Dad.

Jamie hugs him and he kisses the top of her head.

"Now, you'll be faced with this every day," he tells her. "But you shouldn't eat it every day because if you do you'll be too fat to get on the plane to come home. Have something like this instead." He throws something in the air and Jamie catches it.

"A Pop-Tart? Gee, thanks," she says.

Dad kisses her again and then sits down to dish out the food.

"So, are you excited?" Mum asks Jamie.

"Yeah," Jamie says, pushing Dad's hand away as he tries to pile more and more food on her plate. "Excited and nervous."

"That's the best thing," Dad says. "If you're not scared in life, you're not doing it right. Which reminds me," he winks at Jamie and turns to me. "What's this about you having a boy in your room last night?"

"Da-ad!" I say and the rest of my family laughs.

"It wasn't just any boy," Jamie says. "It was Dan Bailey."

"Dan Bailey!" Mum says. Thanks to Jamie's big mouth, she knows all about my crush. "So? Tell all."

"There's nothing to tell," I say. And I really don't want to talk about it until I've talked to Jamie about Jack.

"Come on!" Dad says. "Was there kissing?"

"God, Dad," I say, stuffing bacon into my mouth. "I am not talking about this with you!"

"Me and Jack split up," Jamie says and I almost choke on my bacon. Seriously. You know when you get a bit of gristle caught in your throat and you do that hacking noise like you've swallowed a fur ball?

"Woah!" Jamie says as Mum smacks me between the shoulder blades and I spit the remains of the bacon out on my plate. "If Dan Bailey could see you now!"

"So what happened?" Mum asks.

"Della was too busy daydreaming about Dan Bailey to chew?" Jamie says, wrinkling her nose at the carnage on my plate.

"No," Mum says. "What happened with you and Jack?"

"Oh, right," my sister says. "I finished with him. You know, I'm going away for the summer and I'm not interested in a long distance relationship, and all that crap."

"And they say romance is dead," my dad says.

I see Mum and Dad look at each other and

I think they're probably relieved, even though they would never say. I think they worried Jamie would be out in California, pining for her boyfriend. Some hope! She's more selfish than that. She obviously binned Jack to leave the way clear for any surfer boys she might meet. Likes to keep her options open, does Jamie.

I bet Jack was devastated, though. He was mad about her. They always are. Still, it means I can stop worrying about telling her. She finished with him and he tried it on with her sister to get back at her. Pathetic. Dan was right – he's an arsehole. And I'm free to think about Dan. Yay!

I can't help wondering what's going to happen. With Dan, I mean. I know Maddy will tell me not to get my hopes up, that boys are famously temperamental and unreliable, that it might have just been a one-night thing. But the whole summer is ahead of us and maybe I'll get to spend it with Dan...when I'm not working at the deli, that is.

But he can meet me after work, we can have a coffee together and then go to the park and sit in the sun (if there is any sun) or we could maybe even get the train to the coast, to Blackpool or Lytham. Go to the fair, sit on the beach. Or we could go into Manchester. Maybe we'll go out for dinner. I might meet his family. It could be the best summer ever.

Like something out of a romance novel.

I can't find it. I can't find my diary. I've looked
everywhere it could possibly be and it's not there.
Anywhere.

Yesterday, after breakfast, we took Jamie to the
airport and the whole way there I tuned out of
the three of them talking about how amazing
California was going to be and what a great
opportunity and how it was the perfect beginning
to Jamie's university 'career' etc. etc. and tried to
concentrate hard enough to remember where I'd
had my diary last.

I can remember sitting on my bed, a couple of

hours before the party, and writing about how I was jealous that Jamie was going away for the summer, but that my perfect summer would come. I remember that I left the pen tucked between the pages – which I wouldn't normally do because then it makes a strange bulge in the middle of the book – but I was planning to write more. Except I didn't because then Maddy turned up.

And I can't remember hiding it.

Except I must've done. I just *must* have.

There's no other explanation.

OK. There is one other explanation.

And that is that I left my diary on my bedside table for dozens of virtual strangers to read at their leisure.

Honestly, I can't even think about that. It's got to turn up. If I think of people at the party reading it, I get a feeling like I've swallowed something hot and spiky. It makes me bend over and clutch my stomach.

But what makes me feel even worse is the thought that Dan might have seen it. No, actually, that's not the worst thing. The worst thing is that

Dan might have taken it.

I have this image in my head of Dan and Gemima Lee sitting in his room, reading my diary to each other and laughing. She'd have bare feet and her toenails would be perfectly manicured. He'd just be in pyjama bottoms and a T-shirt because they're so comfortable together.

I can even hear her: "Oh, will Dan Bailey ever look at me?! Even if he knew who I was, he'd probably like my sister better, waah waah waah!"

And Dan just looking at her. And then rolling on top of her. And then...

OK, well it would explain a lot, wouldn't it? It would explain why Dan suddenly showed an interest in me after all these years. I knew it couldn't be real. I knew he had to be setting me up for something. But then for a while, last night, I thought... Well, it doesn't matter what I thought, does it? Not now that he and Gemima Lee are most likely shagging on top of my diary.

And what pisses me off even more is that means my first real kiss (that I'm counting) is ruined. I'll never be able to think of it as a nice thing, an exciting thing, one of those life-defining moments people are always talking about. Instead, I've got my sister's idiot ex shoving his tongue in my mouth, and then the boy I've been mad about for years kissing me just so he could humiliate me. But, oh no, it's even worse than that, isn't it? Because I kissed him. I am such a loser.

Once Jamie's gone – and Mum and Dad have stopped wailing about how hard it is to set your children free – everything goes back to normal. Well, as normal as it can be, knowing that someone, somewhere, is reading my private thoughts. But I go back to work at the deli.

As much as I'd like to have the summer off, I do like working here. I mean, at least it's my family's business and I'm not working in McDonald's or somewhere. Maddy's got a job in Primark and, much as I love Primark, I wouldn't want to work there, either. Here, I've got freedom.

Mum and Dad always spend a year working in the latest deli they open to build it up. They opened another one in Chorlton earlier this year, so they're hardly ever at this branch. I don't have to worry about being late (although I do try not to be) and, if I need to, I can leave early. Plus if anyone comes in that I want to avoid I can hide in the back until they've gone.

This morning I thought I was going to be opening up, but when I get there the shutters have already been raised and I can see lights on in the back. I unlock the door, shouting, "Morning!" as I go in.

Bob's head pops up from behind the chiller cabinet and makes me jump. "What are you doing?" I ask him.

"Dropped a load of change when I was cashing up last night and I'm still a few quid short. Thought I could find it without anyone noticing, but apparently not."

Stretching up to his full six foot four, he runs a hand through his shaggy hair. Mum and Dad have tried to get him to stop doing that – it's unhygienic, particularly for a chef – but they don't have a hope because he doesn't even know he's doing it. They do occasionally threaten him with a hairnet though, which is something I for one would pay to see.

"How much are you short?" I ask him.

"Only, like, £3.50, £3.75."

"Oh, don't worry about it!" I say.

"Easy for you to say, bosses' daughter," he says, as he lifts the till with one massive hand and gropes underneath it with the other. "A-ha!" He brandishes a pound coin.

"Oh, shut up. You know they wouldn't bother. These things happen."

"Well, it's less than three quid now. I think I'll give up until later."

I roll my eyes. I used to think Bob was just incredibly conscientious, but it's not that; he's got a thing about losing things. It freaks him out. He can't relax until he's found anything he's lost, no matter how unimportant. Once, he arrived at work, realised he'd dropped his beanie hat somewhere on the twenty minute journey and went out on his breaks and his lunch looking for it. He finally found it on his front path when he got home that night; it'd taken him over an hour to get home since he'd practically done a fingertip search the whole way.

I could tell him about my diary, but it could go one of two ways:

1. He'd be like a sniffer dog and comb the town searching for it.

2. He'd realise instantly it was stolen, not lost, and it'd give him a twitch so bad he wouldn't be able to slice the salami for a week. And that's not a euphemism by the way – slicing the salami is precision work. He likes to go to a 'zen' place when he does it.

As I brush up the front of the shop again (we do it at night, but it's amazing how dusty it can get when there's no one even here) Bob makes me a carrot and apple smoothie (I know it doesn't sound very nice, but it's delicious) and, once I've had a sip, I switch on all the lights, turn the 'Closed' sign to 'Open' and unlock the door.

At lunchtime, Maddy arrives, completely out of breath. As soon as she's through the door, she checks her watch. "Seven minutes, door to door."

"Great!" I say, grinning.

"So I need to leave at ten-to, if I want time for

a wee." She goes into the back of the deli, stashes her bag and her jacket, then sits on one of the barstools in the window. "How's it going?"

"Fine, yeah. Same as usual. How about you?"

"OK, yeah. Busy. Paisley, the girl I'm working with—"

"Paisley?!"

"I know! Anyway, she knows Alison Stevens through her sister or something and she knows what was on the note!"

"No way!"

Alison Stevens' note is a legend at our school. She was in Jamie's year, but she got suspended after a teacher confiscated a note she was passing round in a physics lesson. Then she got pregnant and never came back. No one knows what the note said.

"Yep. Listen to this. Paisley doesn't know exactly what it said—"

I roll my eyes. We've heard vague stories before and they've always turned out to be rubbish.

"No, listen! It was about getting fingered—"

I pull another face and Maddy practically shouts, "Listen!"

"It was about getting fingered—"

"Can you stop saying that?"

"If you stop interrupting me, yeah. It was about getting—"

I stick my fingers (ew) in my ears and go "La la la!"

"OK, OK! By...Mr Drew!"

"Shut. Up."

"I know! Can you believe it?"

"Oh my God. That explains a lot."

Mr Drew was one of our favourite teachers. He was really funny and cool, but then he left very suddenly. We'd heard rumours that he'd been having a bit with a student, but as far as I know no one had ever put the two stories together before.

"Makes sense doesn't it?" Maddy says.

"Shit," I say. I'm amazed.

"Anyway, Paisley still sees her – Alison Stevens – sometimes, and she's had another kid."

Alison's first child was a girl named Prada. I *know*.

"Name?"

"Troy. It's a boy," Maddy said with a straight face.

"Oh, hey!" she says, suddenly. "Did you find your diary?"

I told her about it, but, unlike me, she's convinced it's in the house somewhere.

"No," I say.

"God," she says. "So what do you think? Do you think it's going to turn up?"

"No. I think Gemima Lee's got it."

Maddy screws her face up. "Do you think? God, that'd be awful."

"Ha!" I say. "I know."

"So what are you going to do?"

I shrug. "What can I do? Just wait and see, I suppose."

Back home, after work, I'm watching a *Friends* repeat when I hear the phone ring. I don't even think about getting up – how can I? Chandler's about to propose to Monica – and it's not going to be for me anyway. Maddy's just texted me, trying to get me to come out with her and Sid and Leo, but I'm just not in the mood.

I haven't found my diary yet. I'm clearly not going to find it. But I bet I'm going to hear about it. At some point.

The door bursts open and I can feel Mum's excitement before she even says anything.

"Phone for you!" She's practically hopping up and down. Sometimes she's more like a sister than a mum. An embarrassing sister.

For a minute I have this mad flash that it's the police to tell me they've recovered my diary. You know, they've done a fingertip search of parklands, dredged the river and everything. But just as quickly that thought's gone, and then Mum whispers, "It's Dan Bailey."

My stomach lurches so violently that I actually think for a second I'm going to be sick, but I grab the arms of the chair and the feeling subsides. Dan Bailey. Who may well have my diary. What could he be phoning for? To tell me he's got it? To ask for a ransom? To read particularly embarrassing bits out to me? To say I can have it back, but most of it's stuck to Gemima Lee's arse?

"Come on!" Mum hisses.

I don't know what to do. I don't want to talk to him. But what if... What if he didn't take it? Or what if he did? I'm not going to find out by just sitting here watching TV.

I sigh dramatically and drag myself up out of the

chair. Mum gestures excitedly at the phone on the kitchen wall, as if I've forgotten where it is, then she tiptoes out of the room and ostentatiously shuts the door behind her. Great. Privacy.

"Hello?"

"Hi. Della?"

Even though I knew it was him on the phone, I'm still surprised to hear his voice. My knees wobble. I pull over a dining chair and drop into it.

"Yeah, it's me. Hi," I say. My voice doesn't sound like me.

"So it was good the other night," he says.

I want to rest my head on the table. I want to go back in time to when he was kissing me and I still had my diary. I want to hang up the phone. I want to ask him outright about the diary. But I don't do any of these things. I just say, "Yeah."

"So, I was wondering if you wanted to come out with me one night. They haven't got any of those eighties nights planned at the moment, I checked. So what about the cinema?"

"Oh, right." To the cinema. With Dan Bailey. Without my diary. Not that I would have taken it with me even if I...oh, you know what I mean. I don't know what to do.

"So do you?" I can hear him smiling. I bet he thinks I'm just bowled over to be talking to him. I bet he thinks I'm thinking I'm the luckiest girl alive. Or maybe he thinks Maddy's here and I'm miming the conversation to her.

"Just let me think," I say, and he laughs.

OK, so what's the worst that could happen? I could go to the cinema and be stood up. By Dan Bailey. Who I've loved for years. Or I could go and he could turn up with my diary and laugh in my face. Or I could go and he could turn up and not know anything about my diary at all. But if I don't go, I'll never know.

"OK," I say.

"OK?" He actually sounds pleased.

"Yeah."

"Great. So how's Friday night?"

Friday night? Two days away. Still time for my diary to miraculously reappear. Or for the police to find it on a train headed for Mexico. Or something.

"Friday's fine."

*

I go online to message Maddy and tell her about the date, but when I log in to my email I'm amazed to find there's a message from Jamie. I didn't expect it at all. I thought I'd find out how she was getting on through Mum and Dad. I mean, we never really talked when she was home, so why would she keep me updated when she was away?

Hey D

So this is all a bit mad. I'm here. It's hot and it looks like California. It's the O.C. bitch! Well, it's not really, but it might as well be. I've met two guys already – Aidan and Nathan. Aidan's American and seems a bit full of himself. Nathan's from Birmingham and he's gorgeous. He could be the one, if you know what I mean...!

The hotel kind of looks like a sandcastle, but it's pretty posh and it's right on the beach. My room's shit – it looks like it's been made from the bit left over when they'd finished all the real rooms – but I'm not going to be spending much time here anyway, I shouldn't think.

There's a welcome party on the beach tonight. I'm wearing tiny cut-offs and that pink sequinned vest – you know, the same as yours? I'm not saying tonight's the night with Nathan, but I'm definitely going to put the idea in his head, you know?

Wish me luck!

J x

OK, so what is she going on about? She doesn't call me 'D'. She would never speak to me like that. That's, like, the longest conversation we've had in years, probably. Was she drunk? Is it drugs? I mean, I know they're into all that in California, but she's only been there a couple of days! And what sequinned vest? I haven't got a sequinned vest, I— Oh. Hang on. You know who has got a sequinned vest the same as Jamie's? Her friend, Danielle.

D for Danielle. So, she meant to send it to Dani, but she sent it to me instead. Interesting.

A couple of minutes later, there's another message:

Della

I think I sent an email to you that was supposed to be for Danielle. I assume you read it, so I suppose all I can say is that it wasn't for you and so you should ignore everything that was in it.

Anyway, hope things are OK with you. It's great here – hot and hard work, but I'm having a good time.

Say hello to mum and dad – will ring them when I get a chance.

Jamie x

Wow. She doesn't waste her time with the warm and fuzzies, does she? I know she put a kiss at the end, but she's been doing that on everything since she was about eight. Apparently she did it on an exam paper once. At first I'm not even going to bother replying and then I think, what the hell, and type:

58

Jamie

I don't know. There's a lot of stuff in that email that I'll find hard to keep to myself. I mean, Nathan could be 'the one'. The one what? Your one true love? Are you going to marry him and move to Birmingham?

And you're not going to be spending much time in your hotel? I think mum and dad would be interested to hear that. I mean, part of the reason they paid for you to go was that you'd be in the hotel with the other summer workers, not who-knows-where with who-knows-who...

Della x

I wait for a few minutes, expecting an abusive email in return, but she must have lost interest because nothing comes through.

5

"She's a total dope," Maddy says, as she pulls every item of clothing out of my second drawer and drops it on my bed. She's talking about Paisley. "Do you know what she said today? She'd written a note for me about some stock problem and it was all in capitals. So then she said, 'I can only write in capitals' and I was like, 'Oh really, that's interesting'. And then she said, 'I can type in normal letters'."

I laugh. "Oh bless. Maybe she's got other skills."

"Yeah, well, judging by the amount of lads waiting for her after work tonight, she definitely has. Even Russ was there." Maddy pulls a horrified face. She had a bit of a one-party fling with Russ last summer and she's never recovered. Or drunk tequila again. He was a bit of an over-enthusiastic kisser. If she wanted her nostrils licked, she said, she'd do it herself.

She's separating my clothes into piles. Well, to be clear, she's separated my clothes into one big pile, and one sparkly top.

"Honestly, Della," she says. "If you're going to start" – she stops to do air quotes – "'dating', you're going to need better clothes. The charity shop would reject this lot. Take it to the recycling bin in Asda's car park. But don't be surprised if it coughs them back up."

"What's wrong with this?" I ask, holding up a black top with lace on the shoulders and a low neck. "You were with me when I bought this!"

"Yeah. And when was it?" She snatches it out of my hands. "About four years ago?" She fiddles with it until she finds a tear in the seam. "See? It's knackered." She pulls out the label. "And it's age 11-12!"

"Fine. So I'll wear that." I point at the sparkly top.

"God, no. Too much for a first date. You'll have to buy something new."

"No money. Haven't been paid yet, and I spent all my savings on my phone."

"We'll have to nick something from Jamie's wardrobe." Maddy is already heading towards my sister's room.

"I think she took everything with her," I say. "And she'd kill us both if she knew we were in here."

My sister's room is much, much tidier than when she was at home. I don't know whether she did it before she went or if Mum's been and done it since she left. I bet she couldn't resist it. It still smells of Thierry Mugler's Angel though.

"Have you looked in here for your diary?" Maddy asks me. "Someone could've hidden it in here...or Jamie might've taken it?"

I know this is hard to believe, but I hadn't even thought of looking in Jamie's room. I think I was so freaked out that I convinced myself it had been taken and didn't even consider the other options. What an idiot. I suppose it could be anywhere in the house. Even my parents' room. Gah. I'm so not searching there. Me and Maddy looked in my mum's top drawer for something once (OK, not 'something' – bras; we were too young to have our own and we just fancied wearing them to see what it was like) and all I'm saying is that, when I close my eyes, I still see its little pink bunny face.

"Where do you think she'd hide it?" Maddy asks as I suppress a shudder.

"I don't know... Bedside drawer? I mean, I don't think she'd hide it. It'd kind of be enough that she'd taken it."

"Me or you?" Maddy asks, nodding at the drawer.

I have to say, I'm a bit scared to open it after...the last time. "You do it," I say.

Maddy pulls the drawer open and screams, making me jump. I mean, really, my feet came off the ground. Almost immediately I know that she's taking the piss because she falls on the bed laughing. "Your face!" she screeches.

"Shut up," I say and peer into the drawer. The first thing I notice is the Marc Jacobs Daisy Perfume Ring I bought Jamie for Christmas. "Oh, charming," I say and Maddy sits up, still giggling. "She asked for this!"

"Can I have it?" Maddy asks, lifting it out of the drawer.

I knock it out of her hand. "No! We can't take anything. She's probably got photos of everything in this room!"

Maddy laughs, "She's not that bad."

"Pft! You don't know her as well as me."

"Ooh! Condoms!" Maddy hoots. She waves them at me. "Can I have these?"

"Jesus, no! You can't have anything. Why don't you look for clothes and I'll look for my diary. You're stressing me right out."

Maddy opens Jamie's wardrobe and starts ferreting around. I glance over and it looks like slim pickings.

I poke around some more in Jamie's drawer, but there's no sign of my diary. There's Berocca vitamin powder, more condoms, a passport photo of Jack and, underneath it, a Post-it note with "I will always love you" written on it. It's not Jamie's writing, but I'm not sure it's Jack's either. I hold it up and show it to

Maddy, but then I'm sorry because she immediately starts singing the Whitney Houston song. Badly.

"Hey!" I say. "Hang on. What do you need condoms for? You're on the pill, aren't you?"

Maddy glances over and I think she's almost blushing. It takes a lot to make her blush and so I'm immediately suspicious.

"Is everything OK with you and Sid?" I ask.

"Yeah, it's OK. I was just joking about the condoms."

"Are you sure?"

"Yeah," she says. But then she sits down heavily on the bed. "I'm just a bit bored, I think. It's like – he says that we're perfect for each other, so what's the point in thinking about anyone else? Actually, he said, 'I'd never get anyone better than you.' Which you can take two ways, can't you?"

I laugh.

"But I don't know. He's great, and I love him, but I can't help thinking..."

"What?"

"That there might be..." She looks over at me and her eyes are full of tears. "Something better."

"Oh, Mads," I say. "But why?"

"I don't know. I'm just being stupid."

"Is there someone else?"

"No," she says. Too quickly, if you ask me.

"Really?"

"No, not really..."

"Not really?"

"Well..." She sits up straight and stares at me really intently and, to be honest, even though she's my best friend and I love her and everything, I feel a bit scared. It even flashes into my mind that she's going to say Dan. Dan Bailey.

"I've been thinking about Leo."

"Leo," I say, but I'm not sure it's audible.

"Yeah. I mean, he spends all his time with us and I just wonder sometimes if I'd be better off with him than Sid. He's more my type, you know?"

"How can he be more your type? You've been with Sid for years!"

"Yeah, but Sid... Sid's great, but, you know?"

I shake my head. "No. I don't know."

"OK, but... Don't freak out, OK?"

I nod.

"In bed, Sid's a bit...boring."

"Boring," I repeat. Or possibly just mouth since I don't actually hear the word come out.

"It's always the same, you know?"

"No, I don't know."

"No." She looks down at her hands and then up at me. "Should we stop talking about this?"

"No, no. You're my friend. You can tell me anything. Even if it's going to give me nightmares, and means I'll never be able to look Sid in the face again."

"No, it's nothing bad. It's just, like, it's always the same with him. It's like he thinks he's got these moves that work and there's no point in trying anything different. And if I ever suggest anything different and, you know, it works, then that's what he does the next time. I just wish he'd mix things up a bit, that's all."

"But how do you know Leo will be any different?" I ask. What I mean is, how does she know anyone's different? How does she know that isn't what sex is like?

"I don't. But I don't think everyone would be so obsessed with sex if that was it, you know?" She pauses for a minute, then says, "Do you think I'm really bad for fancying Leo?"

"No!" I say. "There's nothing wrong with noticing that another boy's good-looking is there? I mean, my mum's always saying she'd have a go at Johnny Depp, given half the chance. But I don't think Dad's worried she'll actually leave him for him. And, let's face it – she's not going to get the chance, is she? I don't think Johnny Depp spends as much time in Sainsbury's as my mum does." I'm babbling.

Maddy laughs and shakes her head. "Anyway, never mind that. Tonight's about you and" – she says it like it's this big announcement – "Dan Bailey!" And then does an 'audience going wild' noise.

I lean over and hug her and we sit in silence for a few seconds, then I say, "I'd better get on with—" and wave at the drawers. Maddy jumps up and heads back to Jamie's wardrobe.

I put everything back in the top drawer, close it, and open the next drawer. It's empty apart from a copy of *Heat* and a few pens. The bottom drawer is empty (apart from some dust and fluff), but when we were little Jamie used to hide stuff underneath the bottom drawer, so I pull it all the way out and put it on the bed next to me. I give a squeal of excitement because there is a book there and, at first, I think it's my diary. I quickly realise it's not; it's not the right size. I lift it out and see that it is *a* diary, but not *my* diary.

"Look," I tell Maddy, holding it up. "Jamie's diary."

"Oooh!" Maddy says, dropping the blue tartan dress she'd been holding. "Can we read it?"

"No! God! Considering the state I'm in over mine, I'm hardly going to read hers."

"Oh, go on! I bet she'd read yours."

"Oh, well that's OK then," I say sarcastically. "No. I'm not reading it."

"Just a little bit?"

"No." But as I go to put it back, I can't resist a quick flick through. I see that she hasn't actually written anything in it, except for her name on the front page. After I've shown Maddy, I put it – and everything else – back. Maddy throws herself backwards on the bed, sighing dramatically.

Maddy doesn't know – in fact, no one knows – that I did actually read some of Jamie's diary once. It was a couple of years ago when we were on holiday in Portugal. As usual, Jamie met a load of lads on the first day and they were all fawning over her. I hadn't met anyone, so I was kind of hanging around with them. A couple of the lads were nice to me, and there was one, Sam, who I really liked. He had tufty hair and he smelled really good (it turned out to be this dodgy aftershave, but I didn't know that at the time). I thought he liked me, and I really liked him.

And then, this one night, we were all down on the beach, and Sam disappeared. He'd been gone about five minutes when I realised that Jamie had disappeared, too. She knew I liked him; I'd been talking about him enough. She said he was a 'spod' and I was welcome to him, and she was going after this much older boy, Fernando, who worked at the hotel. (I'm not sure what his job was, he seemed to spend most of his time having to fake-laugh at the tourists singing that old Abba song to him.)

Anyway, obviously, Jamie had gone off with Sam. I was so upset and I kind of *flipped-out*. I ran back to the hotel, crying. It was really embarrassing because everyone saw, and knew what had happened. I kind of expected Jamie to come after me, but she didn't and she never mentioned it. The next morning, she was just kind of smirky and I couldn't understand it. I didn't know what I'd done to make her be such a bitch to me.

So that afternoon, she went to the pool with the boys (including Sam) and I read her diary. I wanted to know if, deep down inside, she felt bad for what she'd done. But she hadn't. Or, if she had, she hadn't admitted it in her diary either. She'd written about what a 'loser' I was, and how hilarious it was when I went 'boo-hoo-hooing' back to the hotel. I think that was probably when I realised that we'd always be sisters, but we'd probably never be friends.

"Hello!" Maddy shouts. "Earth to Della!"

I look at my best friend – my best friend who is so much nicer than my sister – and smile. "Why are you looking at that dress? I'm not wearing a dress on a first date!"

"Not for you. I was thinking of it for me." Maddy says. She hangs Jamie's dress back up and carries on rummaging. I look vaguely around the room, waiting for my diary to leap out and shout, "There you are! I've been looking for you everywhere!" Yeah, I know, I'm way too attached to my diary.

"Did Jamie leave her Fake Bake?" she asks, as she roots about.

"I haven't seen it," I say.

"She's hardly going to need it in California."

"She probably took it for those first few pasty days," I say, watching Maddy check and disregard each item in my sister's wardrobe.

"Yeah, I hadn't thought about how pasty I'm going to be spending every day in Primark."

"Don't they sell fake tan?" I laugh.

She doesn't dignify me with an answer, saying instead, "How about this with your jeans?" She holds out a short purple kimono type thing with a ruffle on the front.

I pull a face. "It's a bit girlie, isn't it?"

"Newsflash. You're a girl. No, it's nice. It's not too dressy, not too scruffy. It might even make you look like you've got some boobage." She starts undoing the buttons. "Easy access."

She grins, and I snatch the kimono off her. "OK, I'll wear it, just stop talking about my boobs."

I'd arranged to meet Dan in the cafe bar at the cinema. I tried to be a little bit late (but not too late) so that he'd be there first (and I wouldn't be sitting there alone, like a sad-arse), but when I arrive, he's not there.

This place is done up as if it's a proper nightclub, but it's always full of kids taking a break from playing *Dance Dance Revolution* to slurp down some E numbers, before tackling *Grand Theft Auto*.

I get myself a Coke from the bar and sit down (in a seat with a good view of the main door) to wait. All sorts of scenarios have gone through my head leading up to tonight:

- Not only would Dan be there, but also Gemima Lee and loads of their friends, all lined up to laugh at me.
- Dan wouldn't be there.
- Dan is hiding, filming me (being stood up) on his mobile, which he would then post on Facebook.
- Not only would Dan be there, but also Gemima Lee and loads of their friends, all lined up to read from my diary.
- Dan wouldn't turn up, but would instead send some spoddy mate to tell me he'd changed his mind, and I'd end up spending the evening with him instead.
- Dan would turn up and everything would seem to go fine, but then I'd discover that we'd been followed all night by Gemima Lee...who would then put pictures she had taken up on Facebook.

Honestly, dating must have been a lot easier before Facebook and mobiles were invented. Although I guess you still had to worry about being stood up and/or humiliated – probably since the dawn of time.

I bet the first cavewoman sat on a rock, waiting for the first caveman and thinking, "I bet he's not bloody coming!"

I'm halfway through my Coke, and starting to think about getting my mobile out (you're never alone with a mobile), when I see Dan crossing the car park and heading for the double doors.

For a second, I think about legging it, but then I think, well, what have I got to lose? Apart from my dignity. I take a gulp of my Coke so that I don't have to arrange my face into any particular expression, and then he's there, right in front of me, looking flustered.

"I'm so sorry," he says. "I missed the bus so I ran most of the way."

His face is quite red and his hair is damp around the edges, so I believe him. And he looks extremely foxy.

"That's OK," I say and then gulp more Coke.

Dan looks at his watch. "We've got time for a drink – or another drink." He gestures at my glass. "Before the film. What do you think?"

I manage to say, "Yeah, great."

Dan says, "'Nother Coke?" and then he's gone to the bar.

I gaze after him for a second – he's so confident and gorgeous – before turning to watch two lads playing on the air hockey. It's not working properly – not enough air – so they're practically throwing the puck to each other. One of the bouncers will be along in a minute; they don't take any crap in here.

As I predicted, the bouncer's just coming out of the back office when Dan arrives with the drinks and sits down next to me. Stupid me. I'd told myself beforehand to make sure and sit at a table with chairs, to avoid any of that 'where to sit?' awkwardness. But I'd forgotten and sat in a booth, so Dan's had to scoot in right next to me, and now we're sitting side by side. Oh yes, very casual.

"So..." he says.

"Er, yeah," I say. I kind of want to say, "So, this is nice!" but that's the kind of thing my gran would say, so I don't.

"Good party last week," Dan tries.

"Yeah," I agree. I immediately think of my diary

and wonder if I can ask him about it. Can I? I don't know. Let's see.

"Did your sister get away OK?" he asks.

"Yeah. I think she's enjoying herself. She sent me an email by mistake and it sounded like she was having fun."

"By mistake?"

I glance at him, and he's smiling. He's so cute when he smiles.

"Yeah, she meant to send it to her friend, Danielle, but she obviously didn't read the address properly and..." I wave my hand as if to say, "You can guess the rest" but Dan says, "Ah. Della." And I know this is going to sound melodramatic, but when I hear his voice saying my name, I feel like my heart is leaping out of my chest, like in a cartoon. And I think, he can't have taken the diary. He just can't have. There's no way he could have taken the diary and still say my name like that.

Like he's been waiting to say it for years.

So I say, "There was one thing about the party..."

I study his face for a second to see if there are any signs of guilt or smugness or something. And then I leave it another second, in case he cracks under the pressure of my (two second) silence and says, "Yes! It was me! I took your diary!" But no. He's just looking at me patiently with a sweet smile on his face.

"My diary is missing," I say. Then I add, "I don't suppose you saw it?" because otherwise it feels like there's going to be a 'duh duh duhhhhhh!' moment, and I don't want that.

"Shit," he says, simply. His brow furrows and I stare at his lovely eyebrows. "Where did you last see it?"

"I think I must've left it on my bedside table," I say. "Which I know was stupid..."

"Well, yeah, but it was in your room, right? So no one should've gone in there without your permission."

I just nod. I can't think of anything to say. I really don't think it's him. And then I realise I'm looking at his lips and have been for a few seconds more than it's probably acceptable to look at someone's lips if you're not planning on, you know, kissing them.

And then I'm not thinking at all because Dan

Bailey is kissing me. I know I don't have anything to compare it to, but he really is a phenomenal kisser. I mean, I can't imagine that anyone does it better than this. And then his hand is on my back (on top of my top) and his other hand is – oh God – on my neck and I think every single tiny hair on the back of my neck (and on my head, for all I know) has just stood on end and I find myself thinking that it's all gone very quiet – I can't even hear the air hockey tables any more – and I wonder if everyone has stopped what they're doing to watch this kiss.

This perfect kiss.

They hadn't. When we stop kissing and pull apart and smile at each other just for a second – and after I've finished noticing that his lips look kind of pink and plump and biteable and wondering if mine look just as good – then I look around and everything is just as it was before: the skinny guy with the bleached hair and acne is still serving at the bar, the two boys are still throwing the air hockey puck to each other and there's a ginger-haired girl hopping up and down on *Dance Dance Revolution*.

And it just seems wrong. It seems like a kiss that good should have changed everything.

At least it did change one thing. Dan hops out of the booth and holds his hand out to me. I slide across (which I wouldn't ever recommend, since the leather of the seat makes an embarrassing farting noise, which we both pretend not to hear, but at which I'm fairly sure I hear one of the air hockey boys snigger) and take his hand, which is soft and warm and dry.

And even once my feet are on the floor and we're heading for the stairs up to the cinema, he doesn't let go.

I'm out on a date with Dan Bailey and we're holding hands.

He pays for the tickets. He buys drinks and a bag of Maltesers. And then he nips to the loo, giving me a chance to text Maddy: "OMG! This is amazing!" before I have to turn my phone off ready for the film...

...which I don't really see because me and Dan are kissing pretty much the entire time. But he doesn't try to push me to go further, like a lot of boys would. At least, so I've heard.

Dan's hand does, at one point, drift down the front of my top towards my boob, but when I jerk back so violently that I knock the bag of Maltesers onto the floor, I think he realises I'm not quite ready for that kind of thing.

After the film, we walk outside, hand in hand, and then, as we wander over to the taxi rank, he puts his arm around my shoulder. It feels really weird – I can't remember anyone ever having their arm around my shoulder before and I don't really know what to do with my arm, so I just let it dangle – but good weird. The kind of weird I could get used to. Like sushi.

"Hiya, honey," Bob says as I walk into the deli, the following morning. "What've you been up to?"

I imagine telling him exactly what I've been up to and laugh to myself. "Nothing much. You?"

"My eyes in organic honey," he says, rolling his actually honey-free eyes. "I'm making baklava."

"Ooh, yum," I say.

"So, who is he?" Bob asks, without looking up from brushing melted butter onto pastry. The smell in here is heavenly; I've got to eat something.

"Who?" I ask as I take a hunk of Rocky Road ice cream out of the chiller. I know it's early, but it's sweltering outside and I don't see why ice cream can't be a breakfast food. After all, muffins are just cake.

"Whoever's making you grin like a nutter," Bob says.

I laugh as I feel myself blush. "I went out with a boy last night."

"Cute?" he asks.

I laugh. "Very."

"Cool."

"You really can't get away with calling boys 'cute'," I say, pouring myself an iced water to go with my ice cream.

"What should I say then?" he asks. "Hot?"

"God, no. Don't say anything."

"So who is he? How long have you liked him? Where did you go? What did you do? Did you let him—"

I cover my ears. "Stop! I've liked him for ages. We went to the cinema. We saw a film. We went home."

"Was there heavy petting?"

"Seriously," I say, laughing. "Stop now."

I take my breakfast into the shop and Bob shouts,

"Never mind, I'll hear all the details later when Maddy comes in."

I roll my eyes. He's probably right.

We're really busy all morning because it's Saturday, so I don't notice the time until Maddy's standing right in front of me with an excited look on her face.

"Tell me, tell me, tell me!" she says, practically hopping up and down on the spot.

Bob sticks his head out of the kitchen and says, "Baklava?"

"God, yes," Maddy says.

"Frappuccino?"

"Please," Maddy says. "And you should never say that again. You're not in the media. Or Italian."

"God," Bob says. "First I can't say 'cute', now I can't say 'frappuccino'..." He shakes his head. "Same for you, Del?"

I nod and follow Maddy out to sit in the window seats. It's the pre-lunch lull and there's just one customer in the shop who's been browsing the spices for about fifteen minutes, so I think we're OK to talk for a little while.

"So, tell all," Maddy says.

So I do. I tell her everything, including the bit when I asked Dan about my diary.

"So he didn't know anything about it?" she asks.

Bob comes out of the kitchen with our coffees and pastries, then goes to serve the customer who, I see, has chosen one sachet of £1.50 chipotle chilli. After twenty minutes. Jeez.

"Well, that's what I realised," I say. "He didn't say he'd seen it, but he didn't say he hadn't, either. In fact, apart from saying no one should've gone in my room – which, like I said, he did – he didn't say anything either way. And then he kissed me."

Maddy's frowning. "So you think he changed the subject – and kissed you – on purpose?"

"No. I don't know. I know it sounds mad. I mean, he's hardly going to come on a date with me and spend the whole night kissing me—" At this point I hear a "Ha!" from Bob, who is clearly eavesdropping. "Just to cover up the fact that he nicked my diary, is he?"

"It seems unlikely," Maddy says and takes an

enormous bite of her baklava. "Maybe he just wanted you to shut up about your diary 'cos he couldn't wait to kiss you?" she says, spraying pastry flakes everywhere.

I attempt to raise one eyebrow. "Does that sound likely?"

"Well, he clearly likes you, since he spent half of last night with his tongue down your throat." I hear another snort from Bob. "And it seems much more likely than him stealing your diary and then snogging your face off to cover it up. So let's assume he didn't take it unless we find any evidence otherwise, yes?"

I nod. But I'm still not sure. And then Bob appears between us. "So what's this about your diary then?"

I sigh. "I can't find it."

"Do you ever bring it in here?" he says, his brow furrowing. I knew it would freak him out.

"God, no," I say.

"Do you ever take it outside your house?"

"Not really. Not unless we're on holiday or something."

"So you couldn't have just, you know, lost it?"

I shake my head.

"Right. So either it's somewhere in your house or someone nicked it and it's somewhere...in the world?"

"Yes," I say. I feel my heart sinking.

"So the first thing you need to do is search your whole house to make sure it's definitely not there." He scratches his head wildly. He's getting overexcited.

"OK. And then?"

"And then we'll discuss it again."

"Great," I say.

In the afternoon lull – Saturdays are weird, it goes from being chaos to being dead in, like, half-hour intervals – I'm tidying around, alphabetising the spices, picking up bits of litter that customers have left (if you ever feel the need to stick an empty crisp packet down the back of a radiator in a shop, get some help) when Dan comes in.

Dan Bailey.

My first thought is, what do I look like? Which

I know sounds conceited, but the mirror in the shop bathroom is about four inches square, plus it's set so high on the wall that I can only see my face if I stand on tiptoes as far away from it as possible, so I don't usually bother. I scrape my hands through my hair and stick the rubbish in the pocket of my tabard. Oh God, my tabard!

"Hi!" Dan says, and he's smiling that lovely, dimply smile, and I forget for a moment that I'm wearing a tabard, and smile back.

"Are you busy?" he asks.

I look around me as if there are customers milling all around and I just haven't noticed them, and say, "No. Can I get you a coffee or something?" Because, you know, I don't want to assume he's come in here to see me and then have him say he's here for piccalilli or something. (If you don't know what piccalilli is, you're not missing much, honestly. Imagine a jar of radioactive cauliflower vomit and you're on the right track.)

"A cappuccino would be good, thanks," he says and then he sits down in the window in the same seat that I was sitting in with Maddy earlier. I stand and stare at him for a second – he looks really good with the sun shining around him through the window – but then I shake myself and go into the kitchen.

"Is that him?" Bob says. I shush him. Of course, my shushing was actually louder than his speaking so I immediately blush and rattle the coffee cups to cause a distraction.

I nod and put the espresso to one side while I pour the milk into the frothing jug.

"You should go for it, Della," Bob says.

"Why?" I say – or rather, mouth, since he can't hear me over the sound of the milk frothing.

"You should have a bit of fun," he whispers, as I pour the frothy milk onto the espresso. Like my mum, Bob's always on at me to 'have a bit of fun'.

"Why?" I look around for the coffee biscuits. They're supposed to be right here, but Bob keeps moving them – to stop himself from eating them.

"You're too young to spend so much time at home with your parents. When I was seventeen—"

"I know what you were up to when you were seventeen," I say, laughing. He stole his father's credit card and went inter-railing around Europe.

"Not that!" he says. "But I met girls. I had romances. I had fun. When do you have fun?"

"This is fun," I say, poking him in the ribs with the handle of the wooden spoon I'd used to hold down the froth. Bob is extremely ticklish, and giggles like Pooh Bear, before pushing the spoon away and growling, "Gerroff."

"Della," he says, pulling the spoon out of my hand and tapping me on the forehead with it. "There's a cute boy out there. And you're in here, poking a fat chef in the guts with a spoon."

"OK," I say, but I don't move.

"Get out there. Sit with him while he has his coffee. Then tell him you're going down to town to get something, and ask him if he wants to go with you."

"And what should I get?"

"I don't know! Think of something! Sheesh. I can't do everything."

I resist the urge to smack him with the spoon. "Fine. Thanks."

Have you ever had a whispered conversation that you think no one can hear and then you realise that, probably, everyone could hear it? It's like you can still hear the conversation echoing around? Like when you talk on your mobile on a bus or a train and then, when you hang up, you just know everyone was listening to every single word? Well that's the feeling I get when I go back into the shop.

Dan is looking out of the window and fiddling with his mobile, but my and Bob's voices seem to be shimmering in the air. My brain immediately starts to try and remember what was said and how potentially humiliating it was. But when I put Dan's coffee down, and he grins at me, my brain just hums quietly, instead.

"Have you got time to sit down?" he asks, gesturing at the other stool.

I nod and sit down. I think about saying that I've got to go and get something in town. But then I think that if he did overhear Bob suggest that it would be embarrassing and even if he didn't, he might think I mean right this minute, and then I'd end up going on an imaginary errand while Dan Bailey sat alone in my deli.

"I had a really good time last night," he says. He

sips his coffee...which I know is too hot. I actually stick my hand out as if I can stop it before it gets to his mouth, but he doesn't notice and I see him wince and then he says, "Shit. That hurt."

"Sorry," I say, as if it's my fault.

He smiles. "It's not your fault. You'd think I'd learn that fresh coffee is hot, wouldn't you?" He mimes stabbing himself in the hand, "Damn! Knives are sharp!"

"My dad had a cousin who was told not to touch the kettle with his hand in case it was hot, so he tested it with his tongue," I say and Dan winces again. "He's not one of Dad's brightest cousins..." I say. Dan smiles.

There's a short silence, which Dan fills wisely by blowing on his coffee, and then I think to say, "I had a really good time, too."

We smile at each other a bit and then he says, "Did you find your diary?"

"No," I say. "But then I haven't really looked for it." This has got to be a good sign, hasn't it? The fact that he brought it up? He asked me about it... He wouldn't have done that if he was involved in taking it, would he? Unless it was some kind of double bluff. God, I can't even be bothered thinking that. What did I agree? Assume he's not involved until I discover otherwise. OK.

"I'd be turning the house upside down if it was me," Dan says.

"You keep a diary?" I must admit, I'm surprised. Boys don't do diaries, do they?

He laughs. "No. But, I mean, if I did. I had a blog for a while, but it was mostly about graphic design. Not anything, you know, personal."

I think to myself: how does he know my diary is personal? And then I think, well, duh! It's a diary, of course it's personal, and my stomach settles down again. And then rises right back up as some of the things I've written in that diary scroll through my head. I shake my head to clear them away. I bet I don't look mental at all!

Dan dips his biscotti in his coffee and crunches into it.

"So do you like working here?" he asks, looking around the shop. He takes another sip of his coffee.

"Yeah, I do." He's chewing biscotti and so, to fill

the silence, I say, "I think I'd like to run it, one day. But Maddy says I'm just being lazy and I need to think of something better."

Dan laughs. "But if it's what you want?"

"But I don't really know! Maybe I am being lazy and taking the easy option..."

"Well, you don't need to stick with it, do you? It's not as if it's a decision you have to stay with for your entire life, is it? You can start out in the deli and if it turns out you don't love it as much as you thought, then you do something else."

I just stare at him for a minute. I'd literally never thought of it like that. They make such a big deal of it at school that it's as if I'm making a decision I'll be stuck with forever. Dan is smiling at me and I smile back, before saying, "That sounds like a good idea." And then I tell him something I haven't told anyone else – even Maddy. "I'd like it to be a kind of coffee shop/book shop, too. I'd like more seating and maybe some food, and books at the back of the shop."

"Sounds great," Dan says, and it feels like he really means it. For the first time, it feels like something I could actually do with my life.

Dan finishes his coffee and reaches for his bag (it's a messenger bag, not a man bag, thank goodness).

"Where are you going?" I ask.

"Just for a look around," he says, slipping off his stool. "And I've got to get some stuff for my mum."

"I need to pick up some...lightbulbs," I say. "In town."

"Oh, OK," he says, smiling.

"I just need to hang up my...tabard," I say. How humiliating is that?

I head into the back room. I think Dan knows that I'm just trying to prolong my time with him, but I find that I don't really care. I do think for a minute that he's just being polite, but then I find I don't really care about that either. I just want to get to the kissing. It's very unlike me.

When I go back into the deli, Dan is waiting at the door and smiling at me and my stomach flips. Then I look at Bob, who's grinning like a proud father, and I roll my eyes, but that gives me a warm feeling too. Is this why people like going out with people? Who knew?

I meet Dan at the door, tell Bob I'll be back in twenty, and step outside. After being in the air-conditioned deli all day, the heat hits me straight away, and, oddly enough, I sort of shiver.

We both turn towards the town centre and, as we step off the curb, Dan takes my hand. My head is immediately completely empty. It's as if all my functions and abilities have just transferred themselves to my hand. I hope at the very least I can remember how to walk.

I'm home and messaging Maddy about seeing Dan at lunch, when a pop-up tells me I've got a message on Facebook. At first my stomach does a little flip in case it's Dan friending me, but it's from a name I don't recognise and certainly not someone I remember adding as a friend: the name is Peeps.

I click through and at first I'm not sure what I'm seeing. In fact, weird as it may sound, my body seems to get it before my mind does, because I feel my face start to burn, my hands shake and I get that feeling – you know when you're falling asleep and then you do that jerking thing as if you're really falling? Like that. I grab the sides of my chair because I think for a second I'm actually going to topple off.

There's no message, just a photo. Or rather a scan. A scan of part of a page of my diary. I think for a minute that I'm going to be sick and then I feel like I'm being watched. I look around the room for a second, as if I'm expecting someone to jump out, laughing.

The scan goes blurry as my eyes fill with tears. I sit there doing nothing and then my IM starts pinging and I blink enough to see Maddy's sent me a message:

Madge: U still there?

I don't want to tell her about this yet – I can't deal with it myself, let alone discuss it with anyone else – so I just click the red cross to sign myself out of IM. I find myself staring at the scan again.

I remember the page. I remember writing it and I remember almost tearing it out one day when I suddenly panicked that Jamie or even my mum might read it (although I don't really think my mum ever would). The previous page had been all about Dan Bailey and how much I liked him and fancied him and how he wasn't like other boys and how I wished he was actually interested in me, etc. The usual embarrassing kind of girlie diary stuff.

But the bit whoever it was had scanned was something a bit different. It said, 'But since he's not interested in me and nothing's ever going to happen between us, I'll have to make do with the next best thing: touching myself and pretending it's him.'

I didn't sleep much at all last night. All I could think about was that someone had my diary. And then I'd think about who it could be. During the course of the night, I probably suspected everyone I've ever met. At one point, I was even thinking it could be Maddy.

I felt sick. And restless. I couldn't get comfortable and I kept switching my light on and trying to read. But then I'd find that I'd re-read the same paragraph over and over again, as my mind was going over that sentence from my diary, again and again.

And then I started to wonder who else 'Peeps'

might have sent it to. Just because the message was only addressed to me didn't mean it hadn't gone to anyone else, did it? I mean, for all I knew, Peeps could have sent it to every one of their friends. I even got up to look at Peeps's profile, but they didn't have any other friends listed. Just me. But they could have other accounts, of course.

I thought maybe I could find some clues to who they might be, but their profile was totally generic, barely any detail at all. It made me feel a little worse, if that's possible. If they'd been friends with some of my friends then, yeah, I'd be worried that the scan had been sent to them too, but this anonymous profile gave me the creeps. It just seemed so sinister. Particularly as I've been quite careful about who I've friended on Facebook, because some of my friends have had their accounts hacked after adding someone they didn't actually know. Could someone have hacked into my account and added themselves? Or would it have to be someone who knew me and had access to my computer? Although that would include a lot of people at the party. Who knew who'd been in my room earlier in the evening?

Of course, I did know that Dan had been in my room, so quite a lot of the night was spent worrying – again – that Dan was responsible for the whole thing. Dan and, of course, Gemima. But he seems so lovely and genuine that I just can't really believe that he could be involved. Or at least I don't want to.

I went around and around in circles all night. Trying to think of anything that would give me an idea of who it might be, interspersed with feelings of shame, embarrassment and humiliation so hot that they made me roll onto my stomach and curl my legs up. Oh, and of course, there was the crying. Lots of crying.

I text Maddy and ask if she can come round. She replies saying that she's going out with Sid and Leo and do I want to come out with them instead. I send another text making it quite clear that I'm going nowhere and can she please come round and she says she'll be here in fifteen minutes.

I go downstairs and find my mum and dad sitting at the kitchen table with the papers, croissants, jam, cheese, butter and about seven mugs with various amounts of tea and coffee going cold in them, spread out between them. They each get a fresh cup every time they have another drink. It's so wasteful.

I sit down and my dad looks up from the sport section. "You look terrible! Did you not sleep?"

"Not much, no."

"Lovesick? Is it all over already?"

"Steve!" Mum says and swats him with the magazine.

Dad laughs. "I'm only kidding. Couldn't sleep for thinking about him, eh? Or was he here? Did you sneak him in?"

I roll my eyes. "Of course not."

"Why not?" he says. "Your sister used to. I opened the bathroom door one day and there was some spotty lad in there, bare-arsed."

We all know this story, we've heard it loads of times. It was Will, Jamie's boyfriend before Jack and, when I bumped into him in the hall as he tried to sneak out, I don't think I've ever seen anyone so embarrassed in all my life. (Although I imagine that, last night, I came close to it.) He never came to the house again and, if any of us so much as saw him in the street, he'd blush bright red and scurry away. Jamie always insisted nothing had been going on and she hadn't even known Will had taken his clothes off until she heard dad screaming (screaming...and then screaming with laughter). None of us believed her, of course, and Dad started leaving condoms all around the house until she completely flipped out at him and Mum made him stop.

Tutting at my dad, Mum passes me a croissant, a knife and the butter dish. For a minute I think I can't eat anything, but then I realise I'm really hungry and can't shove it in my mouth quickly enough.

Mum pours me a cup of coffee with – and she always does this – loads of milk (she's worried that too much coffee might shrivel my ovaries or something) and then we all go back to reading the paper.

I pick the travel pages and start fantasising about getting as far away from whoever has my diary as possible. Yeah, I'd have to leave my family and friends and Dan, but it would be worth it to not have this hanging over my head any more. I flick through the paper: Malawi? Australia? Italy? Any of them would do. If only I wasn't too young to go. And if only I had some money. For a minute I'm so envious of Jamie I could throw up. My mouth dries up entirely and I have to swig my coffee to wash the croissant down and, even then, chunks of it are stuck to the roof of my mouth.

Wondering how much longer Maddy's going to be, I glance at the clock and, as I do, the doorbell rings. I jump up so fast I almost knock my coffee over and Mum and Dad both look up.

"All right!" Dad says. "Hold your equines!" It's one of his catchphrases.

I let Maddy in and we head straight up to my room. As we're going up the stairs, she says, "Is everything OK? Have you found your diary?"

I shush her until we get to my room and then sit on my bed and find myself crying. Again.

Maddy hugs me until I stop and then says, "What's happened? Is it Dan?"

I shake my head. I don't know whether to show

her the message, or tell her, or what. I know I need to, but I'm just so embarrassed. Eventually I just boot the computer up and let her read it for herself.

When she turns back, she looks absolutely furious. You know when it says in books about people's eyes flashing with fury? Well, Maddy's really are. She looks a bit scary, actually.

"Who's done this?" she says.

"I don't know. I was awake all night trying to think of who it could be."

"Who's 'Peeps'?"

"I don't know. They've got no other friends, and I don't remember friending them. I was wondering if someone had hacked into my account. I don't know."

"Can you contact Facebook and ask them for the details?"

"I don't know. Can you?"

"I bet you can. This is harassment. I think you should tell your parents."

"No," I say immediately. "They'd just worry."

"Or they could sort it out."

"Or they might make things worse. Maybe this is it. Maybe I'm not going to hear any more about it."

Maddy does her one-raised-eyebrow thing.

"Yeah, OK," I say. "But not just yet. I'd rather just wait and see what happens."

"OK. But I'm not going to let you wait too long."

We sit in silence for a few minutes, which is very unlike us. Maddy says, "Do you fancy meeting up with Sid and Leo?" I start to reply, but she puts her hand up. "I know you're not in the mood, but it'll take your mind off it. What else are you going to do? Sit here stewing over it?"

"Yeah, OK," I say. "Where are they?"

"Bowlplex."

I pull a face.

"Yeah, I know," she says. "What can I say? Our options were limited. It was that or church."

I laugh. None of us ever goes to church. But Sid's parents do. Religiously, as he always jokes.

I tell Mum and Dad that we're off out. We decide to walk to Bowlplex; as Maddy says, we might well miss the bowling and get there in time for lunch, which would be the best-case scenario.

As we walk, Maddy talks a lot about work and I talk about Dan. I know she's trying to take my mind off the diary and – occasionally, for a few minutes – I do stop thinking about it. But when I remember it's like a punch in the stomach. Eventually, just as we reach King Street, I can't take it any more and it bursts out: "Who hates me so much?"

Maddy links her arm through mine. "I've no idea."

"Have you never heard anything? In school? Any rumours? Anyone slagging me off?"

"No."

"Honestly?" Maddy's more popular than me and I feel like she would know if anyone had it in for me.

"No, really. No one's ever really seemed that bothered about you!"

I laugh bitterly. "Thanks!"

"No, you know what I mean. You're one of the middling ones – not too popular, not too dorky. Just, you know, you."

"So it's got to be Gemima Lee then, hasn't it?"

"Honestly, I can't think of who else it could be."

"So what should I do?"

"Confront her?"

I actually almost shudder at the thought. I can't

stand confrontation and I really can't stand Gemima Lee. It's much more likely that I would clam up, freak out and she would just slaughter me. The only person I've ever had proper rows with – and, when we were younger, physical fights – is my sister. And I really don't want to have a hair-pulling, scratch fight with Gemima Lee!

"Maybe you should ask Dan about it first," Maddy says, as we walk under the railway bridge.

"About the diary?" I say.

"No, about Gemima. You could ask him if he thought she had anything to do with it. I mean, we might just be reading too much into it. I know she was a cow at the party, but it's possible that's just 'cos you were there and she wouldn't normally give you a second thought."

"I don't know," I say.

"Plus you could do with knowing if she and Dan have ever had a thing."

"Gah!" I say, stopping dead halfway across the zebra crossing. Maddy drags me across the road. "I don't even want to think about that!"

"Well, you know, everyone thought they were

a couple, and I guess it'd make a difference if they were."

"In what way?"

"Well, she might hate you for being with him now..."

"Great." We walk in silence a bit further and I can tell she's still thinking. "What?" I say.

"What?"

"What else?"

She looks at me as if butter wouldn't melt, which just makes me more suspicious. "What!"

"Oh, you know. Maybe they had a row and now he's trying to make her jealous."

Dense as I am, it takes a moment for me to get what she means. "With me?"

She drags me across another road.

"Oh my God, that'll be it!"

"What?" she says.

"That'll be it exactly. I mean, I've been wondering why he's suddenly interested in me out of the blue, after all these years. That must be it!"

"No," Maddy says. "That's not necessarily it. He might just have realised he likes you."

"Yeah, right. What's more likely? I knew it. I knew it'd be something like this!"

"Oh, come on, Del," Maddy says, as we walk up the hill to the cinema. "It was just an idea. You can't assume that's it."

"But what if it is? I stop seeing Dan, he goes back to Gemima, I get my diary back."

"But you like Dan."

"Only if he likes me."

"You only like him if he likes you? You've liked him for years!"

"You know what I mean. If that's the reason he's with me, I don't want to be with him. Obviously."

"But these are all assumptions. You can't bin him on the off-chance we're right."

We push open the doors and walk through the bar where I met Dan before going to the cinema the other night. Maddy puts her arm around my shoulder and squeezes.

"I'm just tired of thinking about it all," I say. "If I stop seeing Dan and it all goes away it'll be worth it."

"But what if you stop seeing Dan and it doesn't go

away. Then you're still being harassed and you've binned Dan for no reason. You need to talk to him."

Maddy goes to find Sid and Leo while I wait by the cashier to see if it's worth us paying for a game.

"They've just booked another," Maddy says, as she gets back. We pay, change into the deeply unflattering (and not all that fragrant) bowling shoes and join Sid and Leo in their lane.

Even though it's late Sunday morning, the Bowlplex is like a club – massively loud music (*Girls Aloud*, mostly) and ultraviolet lighting that makes me glad I'm not wearing a white bra under my black top like a couple of girls a few lanes down. There's even a DJ shouting inane crap like, "Now everyone scream!" And, even sadder, some of the girls do.

Maddy and I sit down and wait for our turn. Leo looks gorgeous. He's wearing a white T-shirt and jeans (and, thanks to the lighting, his T-shirt looks like something off a Persil advert) and you can see the muscles in his arms moving as he rolls the ball. I've never thought of bowling as particularly sexy before, but...yum.

Sid's turn and he's...not so sexy. Nor is he very good at it. His ball smashes down on the lane as if he's going to crack it and the man in the next lane winces. Sid doesn't care though, when he turns around he's laughing. He comes straight over and kisses Maddy, then he ruffles my hair and I tell him to piss off.

"Della's having a bad day," Maddy says, or rather shouts.

I pull a face at her and she shrugs. "He might have some advice."

Not right now he doesn't. He pulls me and Maddy to our feet and we go over to join in the bowling.

Half an hour later – Leo won, Maddy came second, I was third, and Sid last – we're sitting in the cafe and Maddy's telling the boys about my predicament to see if they have any suggestions of who it could be. Thankfully, she doesn't tell them what my diary actually says (she did suggest it, but I said no way), but she tells them everything else, including our theory about Dan and Gemima.

"I'm not sure about that," Sid says, glancing at Leo who seems very interested in his burger. Sid elbows him and he looks up at us. He really is gorgeous. His eyes are like Maltesers and his skin's like Caramac (stress makes me chocolate–obsessed).

"I've been out with Gemima a couple of times," he says, and I actually hear Maddy gasp. I glance at her because I think – hello! – her boyfriend is right there, but she's just staring at Leo with her mouth hanging open.

"So has she said anything about Dan?" I ask. "Or me?"

"Not really, no," he says. He's blushing (which actually makes him look more gorgeous, which begs the question, why does blushing make me just look sweaty and weird?) and he takes a massive bite of his burger. Too massive, it's going to take him a while to get that down – which was probably his plan. Maddy's mouth is still hanging open so I kick her under the table.

"What do you mean 'not really'?" she says, sounding really pissed off. I try and kick her again, but she's moved her leg.

We all sit in silence while Leo finishes his mouthful. It's not uncomfortable at all, oh, no.

Eventually he stops chewing and says, "I mean, she's mentioned Dan because they're mates. But she hasn't mentioned Del."

"Well, she's hardly going to say, 'Hey, guess what, I nicked Della's diary and put it on Facebook?' is she?" Maddy says, still with *that* tone. I look at Sid, but he's munching away on his burger, apparently oblivious that his girlfriend is really pissed off with another boy.

"So, when have you been out with her, anyway?" Maddy says to Leo. I feel myself starting to blush. It's like I'm in the middle of a domestic, but Maddy and Leo aren't even a couple! Leo just looks at Maddy for a few seconds. Then she says, "I mean, you didn't say." Her voice is almost back to normal. Well, it sounds a bit wobbly, but she doesn't sound angry any more. "You know, we're not big fans of Gemima's."

"No, I know," Leo says. "But she's OK, really. When you get her on her own."

Sid sniggers and Maddy shoots him daggers, so I decide to change the subject. Well, I would if I could think of anything to say. Thankfully, Sid comes to my rescue. He says, "We should go on a triple date." And then he laughs.

I actually laugh too because the idea of it is so awful.

When I get home, Mum says that Dan has phoned. She seems very excited (but that may be because she and Dad have already started on their traditional Sunday night bottle of wine – at four in the afternoon).

"He seems like a really nice lad," she says.

My dad winks at me. The phone rings and Dad grabs it, obviously hoping for the chance to speak to Dan himself, and no doubt say something to embarrass me. He has no idea! But I guess straight away that it's not Dan, it's Jamie. I know this because Dad says, "Jesus! You still alive?" Mum rolls her eyes and pours herself some more wine.

I go up to my room and text Maddy to ask her what the deal was with Leo. My mobile rings almost immediately.

"Can I come round?" Maddy asks. She sounds tearful, which is very unlike her.

"Course. Are you OK?"

"Sort of. See you in ten." She hangs up. When I came home, Maddy and Sid were meant to be going back to her house, so I hope they haven't had a row or anything. I mean, I wouldn't be surprised if they had, after the whole scene in the cafe, but I'd hate for them to fall out.

While I'm waiting for her, I go online and, within a couple of minutes (during which I click on Peeps's Facebook profile again, in case she – or, I suppose, he – has added something I can use to work out who it is, but there's still nothing there) I get an IM from Dan.

DantheMan: How are you?
Della: Good, thanx. You?
DantheMan: Good. I phoned before.

Della: Yeah I know. I just got in.

DantheMan: Where've you been?

Della: Bowling. With Maddy, Sid and Leo.

DantheMan: Cool.

I wonder whether to ask him about Gemima and Leo now or wait until I see him again. *If* I see him again. No, I'm definitely going to see him. I think.

Della: I didn't know Leo was seeing Gemima?

DantheMan: Yeah. Been out a couple of times, I think.

I wonder what to say next and then I just think, well, take the bull by the horns. What have I got to lose?

Della: I always thought you and Gemima were together.

DantheMan: LOL! Yeah, people always think that, but no.

Della: How come?

DantheMan: LOL. Don't fancy her. Known her too long.

I was hoping for something more along the lines of,

"Cos she's a total bitch and I'm only friends with her because she's blackmailing me", but you can't have everything I suppose.

Della: Well Leo seems to like her.

That's not necessarily true, but whatever.

DantheMan: I don't know about that.
Della: What do you mean?
DantheMan: I mean I think there's someone else Leo likes.
Della: Yeah? Who?
DantheMan: LOL. I'm saying nothing.
Della: But you've already said something so you should just spill.
DantheMan: Not a chance. ;) Anyway. I rang you and you didn't ring back.
Della: Oh yeah! Sorry.
DantheMan: I wanted to know if you wanted to go out again.
Della: Sounds good.
DantheMan: Cobby's having a party Wednesday night.

I roll my eyes. I've known Cobby since primary school and he's... Well, put it this way: behind his back, most people call him 'Knobby'.

Della: OK, cool.
DantheMan: You want to go?
Della: Yeah. Sounds good.

I am much cooler on IM. At least I think so.

DantheMan: OK, so should I come and pick you up?

I don't get a chance to answer because my door bursts open and Maddy comes in, crying.

"Just hang on one sec," I say to her. I feel slightly panicky because Maddy is not a crier. I turn back to the computer.

Della: Sorry. Got to go. Will ring u.

And I log out.

"What's happened?" I ask Maddy.

She's lying on my bed with her arms over her head. "Nothing, really."

"Oh, come on!" I say. "You don't cry. Usually."

"I'm not crying!"

I snort. She sits up. "I'm not. Look!" She points at her face and, she's right, she's not crying...any more. But it's clear that she has been.

"What's happened?" I ask again.

"Oh, just Sid."

"You have a row?"

"Not really. I was just a bitch to him."

I don't say anything and she notices. Well, she would.

"What?" she says.

"You know."

"No."

"All that business with Leo at Bowlplex."

"What?" She looks genuinely pissed off and, for a second, I'm worried that we're going to fall out. We've only fallen out badly once before in all the years we've been friends, and I'm not in any hurry for it to happen again.

"You know. You seemed like you were pissed off

with Leo when he said he'd been seeing Gemima."

She falls back on the bed again. "Yeah."

"Why?" I ask. And then I think of another question. "Was Sid upset? Because I didn't think he'd even noticed..."

"No. He wasn't upset," she says. She rubs at her eyes. "You're right, he didn't even notice. But then he wouldn't, would he?"

I must admit, I'm confused.

Maddy sighs. "I'm starting to think I could have crawled under the table and unzipped Leo's jeans and Sid would've just carried on eating his chips."

I laugh. "I don't think so."

"Oh, I don't know. He's just so oblivious."

"So you were trying to make Sid jealous?"

She sighs again. "No."

"Well then, what?"

"Well, you know how I said I've been...having... thoughts about Leo."

"Yeah..." I say.

"So, yeah, when he started talking about Gemima I was jealous. Not just because I don't like to think of him with her, but also because I hate her so much. I mean, I'd be jealous if he was with anyone, but especially her!"

"Right," I say. And I understand that totally. There's never been anything between me and Leo, but I really don't like the idea of him and Gemima.

"But also," Maddy says, "I'd kind of started to get the idea that he might be interested in me, and I liked it."

"But—" is as far as I get before Maddy interrupts.

"I know. I know it's ridiculous because I've got Sid. But Sid's just Sid, you know? Like you said, he wouldn't even notice if me and Leo were shagging on the table."

Yeah. I didn't say that, but OK. "So, you liked the idea that he liked you?" I ask.

"Yeah, you know. That whole 'I want you to want me' business."

"Right." And I get that. I do. It's nice to know that someone's interested, even if nothing ever comes of it. Unless it's someone as obnoxious as Jamie's Jack, obviously. "So you didn't actually expect anything to happen with Leo?"

She's quiet for a while. I mean, like, minutes. I'm

trying to think of something to say, but I admit I'm pretty confused. I've always thought of Leo as Sid's friend. Yeah, I know that the three of them spend so much time together, but I've never thought about Leo and Maddy. Not really.

Maddy sniffs and I look at her to see if she's crying again. She's not, she's just sniffing. She wipes her nose on the back of her hand.

"I really like him," she says eventually.

"Leo?" I ask.

"Yeah. I can't stop thinking about him." She rubs her face again. "What am I going to do?"

11

Cobby's house is absolutely massive. It's the biggest house I've ever seen which wasn't on *MTV Cribs*, and it's definitely the biggest house I've ever actually been inside. Maddy says someone told her it's worth almost a million quid, which is absolutely loads around here.

It's up a long, circular driveway, like those you see on, well, *Cribs*. But unlike on *Cribs*, there aren't, like, five Ferraris parked on it. Instead, there are a load of knackered-looking Peugeots and Renaults belonging to all the parents dropping off their kids.

Dan didn't come and pick me up in the end. I was

too worried about introducing him to my parents – I thought it was too soon and Maddy (and she loves my parents!) agreed – so I'm meeting him here.

Neither of us has been to one of Cobby's parties before. Maddy's been asked, but never gone, and I've never even been invited. He has loads of parties because – and this is conjecture – his parents think they might make him popular. And they do – for about a week before he has one, when practically everyone wants to be his friend to get an invitation. But the rest of the time, most people just ignore him. There's nothing really wrong with him, he's just one of those people who's slightly annoying for reasons you can't quite put your finger on.

Anyway, Maddy and I are about to get out of the car when my dad says, "Do you want me to pick you up?"

I look at Maddy. "We could get a cab?"

"You could," Dad says. "Or I could pick you up. What's it to be?"

"What time?" I ask.

"You're both working tomorrow, aren't you?"

Maddy and I both roll our eyes. I can't believe he's pulling the 'school night' thing during the summer holidays.

"Yeah, we are," I say. "So, what? 1am?"

Dad laughs. "Yeah, OK. But you'd better be able to get up tomorrow. So I'll pick you up then."

"It'll be quicker," Maddy says to me.

"Yeah, OK," I tell Dad.

"Glad we got that sorted," he says. "And if I don't turn up, it'll be 'cos I've fallen asleep and you'll have to get a cab."

"Yeah," I say. He always says that, but he's never fallen asleep.

We get out of the car and Dad revs the engine like he always does and zooms off down the drive.

"Honestly, how old does he think he is?" I say.

Maddy laughs. "I love him."

"I know," I say. "You're weird."

We head for the (massive, double) front door and Maddy says, "Hang on" and points down the drive. Sid and Leo are walking up towards us. Sid looks his usual self. He's just wearing jeans and a classic football shirt, but Leo looks really good. He's already caught the sun and he's wearing a black T-shirt, which shows off his tan.

I glance at Maddy and she's got this totally lovesick look on her face. "Mads," I say. "You're drooling."

She smacks my arm. "Shut up!"

But she looks like she's finding it really difficult to turn her head away from Leo and towards, you know, her boyfriend!

Sid and Leo reach the top of the path, and Sid says, "Jesus! Look at this place. It's like something off *Cribs*."

"That's what I was thinking!" I say.

"There's a swimming pool," Leo says. "An indoor one."

"Piss off!" Sid says, laughing.

"Have you been here before?" Maddy asks Leo as we walk to the door.

"Yeah," Leo says.

"With Gemima?" Maddy asks. She sounds fairly cool. I mean, if you didn't know her, you'd think it was an innocent question; but I know her, and I know it's not. Not at all.

"No," Leo says. "I went to primary school with

Cobby. I came here for some football party when we were about ten. He had Tim Flowers doing Beat the Goalie."

"No way!" Sid says.

Leo laughs, "I know. It was magic."

"Wow," Maddy says.

We follow Sid and Leo into the house and I ask Maddy, "Who's Tim Flowers?"

"No idea."

The hallway of Cobby's house is huge. There's a massive staircase going up one side and, of course, there are already loads of people sitting on the steps, draped all over each other. I spot Jamie's ex, Jack, and her friend, Danielle. They're sitting near to each other, but I can't tell if they're together. I wonder for a second if Jamie would care if they were, but then I realise that I don't care, so I follow Maddy down the hall to the kitchen.

We all grab bottles of beer – I don't know if Cobby's parents are here, but I'm guessing not (they must be mad) – and wander in and out of a few of the ridiculously massive rooms, each of which is more crammed with people than the last.

"How many people did he invite?" I ask Sid.

"I think pretty much everyone he knows. He was talking about putting it on Facebook, but he got talked out of that."

When he says Facebook, I feel my stomach drop even before I think about it consciously. My brain leaps to the notion that it could be Cobby who has my diary. But I don't see why he would have; I barely know him. I'm not even sure if he was at our party. Probably not. I certainly didn't invite him, and I doubt Jamie did.

"Hey!" I feel hands on my waist and I turn to see Dan, grinning at me. I grin back and he kisses me quickly on the lips. I see Maddy smile out of the corner of my eye. I also spot Gemima Lee leaving the room. Was she with Dan until I got here? Did she leave because of me?

"I've been looking for you." Dan say, squeezing my waist, making me go a bit weak at the knees. I'm such a cliché!

"Have you seen the pool?" Dan asks, which is good, because I can't think of anything to say other than, "Were you just with Gemima?" and that would make me sound a bit psycho.

I follow him out into the hall – Maddy pinches my bum as I pass her – and then we go through the kitchen and a utility room and into the poolroom. It's not massive, but it's big enough. It's got low lighting, one whole wall of windows onto the garden and there are about thirty people sitting around on beanbags, loungers and the floor.

"You know there'll be people in that pool in a couple of hours," Dan says.

"Yeah. I won't be one of them," I say.

"No?" He laughs. "You don't fancy a midnight swim?"

"God, no."

"That's pretty much always how Cobby's parties end."

"Seriously? What is with his parents?"

"I know. My parents wouldn't even let me have a party. And we haven't got any expensive shit like in this place."

We stay by the pool for a while, chatting with Maddy, Sid and Leo and then Dan asks if I want to go outside. He pulls me to my feet and then, stepping over various legs, we aim for the patio doors. They're already open, so we step through into Cobby's garden. It's really nice. There's a decked area where all the smokers are sitting and also a grassy bit sloping down towards a river.

"I can't believe he's got a river at the bottom of his garden!" I say.

"I know," Dan says. He reaches for my hand and we walk towards it. Everyone else seems to be staying near the house and by the time we get to the bottom of the garden, we're on our own. I look up at the sky. It's quite late and it's been another hot day, so the sky is a lighter blue than usual, but it's still full of stars. We can see them because there are hardly any lights, as the houses around here are so spread out.

There's a bench overlooking the river and Dan sits down, pulling me down next to him. He reaches up and strokes my forehead with his finger.

"You're frowning," he says.

"I was thinking," I say.

"What about?"

"Why you've suddenly taken an interest in me after all these years," I say. I wasn't even sure I was going to say it until I was actually saying it. It just sounds so girlie and needy. "I'm not fishing," I say.

"We could," Dan smiles, pointing at the river.

I smile back with a bit of a grimace, because it was such a rubbish joke. "But, you know, it just seems strange that we never spoke for years and then suddenly you..." I don't know how to finish that sentence.

"I'd seen you around, of course," Dan says. "I always liked you. You seemed cool. You always looked like you didn't care what people thought."

I laugh. "I must be a good actress."

"I like the way you walk."

I've been looking out at the water, but at that I turn to look at Dan. "You like the way I walk?"

He laughs. "Yeah. I saw you from the bus one day – it was a couple of weeks before your party – you were walking down Buncer Lane and I thought at first you had an iPod on or something. You looked like you were walking in time to some music. But when I passed you I noticed you didn't have any earbuds in, or anything. At least, I don't think you did!" He laughs again and I look at his teeth. They're very straight. I can smell beer on his breath. "After that, I kept seeing you around and then I was thinking about you more and more. And then there was the party and I decided I'd, you know..." He raises one eyebrow. "Show you some smooth moves."

I laugh. "OK. I walk like I'm dancing?"

"Not exactly dancing. You walk like there's music in your head."

I smile. It sounds good. It sounds plausible. I want to believe him. Maddy would believe him. Jamie would believe him. Why can't I?

Dan puts his arm around my shoulders and I freeze up.

"What's wrong?" he says.

I drop my head back on the bench and look up at the stars again.

"Someone's got my diary," I say.

"Shit," he says. "How do you know?"

"I got sent a scan of a page on Facebook."

"Shit!" He pulls away and looks at me. He genuinely looks horrified. "Do you know who it is?"

"No."

I glance at him and he's staring at me. "You don't think it's me?"

I look at him. "No. I wasn't sure at first. I thought you might have taken it from my room. I thought maybe that was why you were suddenly interested in me."

"To take your diary? But why?"

"I don't know. It just seemed weird that you turned up in my room – pretty much out of the blue – and then my diary was gone."

"So you said you thought it was me at first. You don't think that now?"

I shake my head.

"Why not?"

"I don't know." I feel myself frowning again, and I don't know how much to say. And then I decide to just put my cards on the table. "I like you. You seem genuine."

"I am," he says. He puts his arm around me again and kisses the side of my head. "I didn't take it. I promise you. I would never do something like that."

I turn towards him, just planning to say

something (I don't know what), but he kisses me. I slide my hand up and around the back of his neck and into his hair. He just feels perfect. And it's such a lovely night. It's hot, but there's a breeze coming off the river. Wow, I'm sitting by a river, the stars are out and I'm kissing the boy I've liked for years!

For a couple of minutes I forget about everything else. But then we stop kissing and I find myself saying, "What about Gemima?" Honestly, I want to slap myself. What is wrong with me?

Dan frowns. "Me and Gemima? I said—"

"No," I say. "Could Gemima have taken my diary?"

Again, he looks genuinely surprised. And then confused. "No. Why? Why would she?"

I shrug. "No particular reason. Just that she seems to hate me."

"I don't think she hates you," he says. "She's never said so to me."

"Well, she's always been a bitch to me."

"I don't think it would be her."

"Really?"

"Yeah. It doesn't seem like her style. Who was the Facebook message from?"

"The username was 'Peeps', but there's no other information. I've emailed Facebook to see if I can get anything else, but I haven't heard anything yet."

"Pepys, like Samuel Pepys?" he says.

I immediately realise that, yes, that's what it's meant to be. Because of the diary. I hadn't even thought of that. We studied Pepys at school, so does that mean it's someone from school? Or would most people associate 'diary' and 'Pepys'?

"I'll be honest," Dan says. "I could kind of see Gem stealing someone's diary..."

I wince at his use of Gem instead of Gemima.

"But if she took it then I think she'd be more likely to read it out at school or something."

"Charming," I say.

"I know. But you know what I mean. She'd want people to realise it was her. She wouldn't do it secretly, she'd want to rub your face in it."

"Well, that's a comfort," I say, and Dan laughs.

"I really don't think it's Gemima," he says.

"OK," I say. "I believe you."

"I've known her since I was five. Our mums are really good friends so we got stuck together before

we were old enough to know any better. And now...
Well, I know she can be a bit of a cow, but she's all
right really. Deep down."

"Really deep down," I say.

He smiles. "Yeah. At the Earth's core, she's cute
as a button."

I smile. "OK," I say.

"Can we get back to kissing now?" he asks.

I laugh. Yeah. We can.

I don't know how long we've been sitting here, but
there's been a lot of kissing. So much that my lips
feel a bit swollen. Someone's coming so I pull back
from Dan and look up the garden. I can see two
people, and at first I think they're coming to the
bottom of the garden for the same reason as me
and Dan. Their voices drift down and I realise it's
Maddy and Leo.

"I don't understand what your problem is," I hear
Leo saying.

Presumably wondering why I've stopped kissing,
Dan starts kissing my neck and I resist the urge to
shush him so I can spy on my best friend.

"I just don't like Gemima Lee!" Maddy says. I feel Dan tense up, so I know he's heard her, too. He looks at me and I don't know what to say, so I just look back at him.

"Is that Maddy?" he whispers. I nod.

"Even if you don't like her, what's it to you who I go out with?" Leo says. "You're with Sid."

"I know," Maddy says, and she sounds like she's trying not to cry. Dan and I stay perfectly still. I feel bad for spying on her, but it's too late to do anything now. If we said anything, she'd know we'd been listening.

"But what if I don't want to be?" Maddy says. I hear her suck in a breath and notice that there's a little red dot by her side – she's smoking.

"What do you mean?" Leo asks.

"I mean, what if I'm not sure I want to be with Sid."

I see Dan's eyes widen, and I'm not surprised.

"You've been with Sid for years," Leo says. His voice has changed. He sounds – I'm not sure – he sounds serious. And a little bit worried.

"I know," Maddy says. "I think that's the problem.

I'm too young to have been with one person for so long."

"So, what?" Leo says. "You want to sow wild oats?"

"I don't know," Maddy says, and I definitely think she's crying. "I don't want to hurt Sid." I see her drop the cigarette and grind it into the ground with her foot.

"Then don't," Leo says.

And then there's silence. I look at Dan and he looks back at me. I hear a mosquito whine past my ear and I resist the urge to slap at it. I look up the garden and at first I think either Maddy or Leo has gone back to the house, but then my eyes adjust and I realise what I'm seeing.

Leo and Maddy are kissing.

12

"Shit," Dan says under his breath.

I'm almost frightened to breathe; I so don't want Maddy (or Leo, for that matter) to know that we're here. I just hope they don't head towards the river or our bench. Of course, they'd have to stop kissing first and it doesn't look like they're going to be doing that any time soon.

"What should we do?" Dan whispers, his lips up against my ear. It sends a vibration straight to what my grandma would call my 'special place'.

I turn and kiss him (and wish I hadn't just thought about my gran). We kiss for a while, but when we stop, Maddy and Leo are *still* at it.

"Jeez," Dan whispers. "We'll have to crawl up the garden, commando-style."

I put my face against his neck so they don't hear me laughing. And then I take a deep breath. His neck smells delish.

I peer up the garden again. "I think they're going," I whisper.

He starts kissing me again and, this time, when we stop, Maddy and Leo are gone.

"Shit," Dan says again.

"I know," I say.

"Did you know about that?"

"No." Because I didn't. Not about the kissing anyway.

"Wow."

"I know. Are you going to tell Gemima?"

He shakes his head. "God, no. I'm not getting involved. That's between the three of them. Well, I mean the four of them. With Sid."

"Shit."

"I know," he says. I smile. "I can't believe it. I thought Maddy and Sid were a together forever kind of a couple."

"Me too," I say.

"And Leo's Sid's best mate."

"Yeah."

"Wow."

"I know."

"That's going to be a tricky one to sort out."

I nod. I actually can't imagine what's going to happen. I don't even want to think about it. I hate the thought of Maddy hurting Sid. I hate the thought of Sid not being around any more. I just can't think about it. What did Scarlett O'Hara say in *Gone With the Wind* (one of my mum's favourite films, even though it's about five hours long)? I'll think about it tomorrow. Or maybe never.

"What time have you got to go?" Dan asks and I lean my head on his shoulder. "One."

"It's ten-to."

"Oh crap, is it?" I start to stand up, but Dan pulls me back down and kisses me again. "I've had a really good time."

"Me too."

"And a bit of intrigue at the end was good, too."

"You won't tell anyone?"

"No, honestly."

"Thanks."

"Are you going to talk to her about it?"

"I should think so."

"Right. You women talk about everything."

I laugh. Women. Right.

Dan stands up and pulls me to my feet and we walk slowly up the garden and back to the house. As we walk through the pool house, I see Danielle and Jack again. They're not doing anything, but they're sitting close together on a lounger. They get up as we get closer.

"Hiya!" Danielle says. She's so pretty. I immediately feel insecure, so I pull my stomach in and hold Dan's hand tighter.

"Hi," I say. Jack nods at me and I nod back. I feel sick just looking at him. "You both know Dan?" I ask.

They smile and say hello to Dan – I notice that Dan doesn't smile at Jack – and then Danielle says, "So, have you heard from Jamie?"

I nod. "Yeah, she sent me an email that she meant to send to you and then she sent me another one slagging me off for not telling her she'd sent the email to me."

Danielle laughs and flicks her hair. Hair flicking. Ugh.

"Yeah, that sounds like Jame."

"You've heard from her though?" I ask.

"Oh yeah," she says. "I'm thinking of maybe going out there for a couple of weeks. It sounds like she's having the best time."

I glance at Jack who is looking straight at me. I don't understand what his game is. He really was mad about Jamie – or at least he seemed to be – so if he is seeing Danielle, it's either to make Jamie jealous or because he sees her as some sort of Jamie substitute. When he realised I wasn't interested in him, did he just go for Danielle instead? Sad.

"We'd better go," Dan says, glancing at the time on his phone. "It's nearly one."

When we finally get outside, after pushing through dozens of other people in the hall, there's no sign of my dad, but Maddy's sitting on the wall opposite. She looks fed up.

"Will I wait with you?" Dan asks.

"If you don't mind," I say.

We cross the driveway and I sit down next to Maddy. Dan sits next to me.

"You OK?" I ask her and she nods.

I glance at Dan and then ask her, "Have you had a good time?"

"Weird time," she says. She sounds tearful, but she's not crying. Dan squeezes my leg and I notice Dad's car coming up the drive.

Dan kisses me quickly. "Should I stay and meet your dad?"

"God, no," I say. "Get inside. Save yourself!"

He laughs and kisses me again. "OK. I'll ring you tomorrow."

Just as Dan goes back in the house, my dad pulls up in front of me and Maddy and we both get in the back of the car.

"Good time?" he asks.

"Great," I say.

"Mads?"

"Not bad," she says.

"It's an amazing house," I say.

I look at Maddy and she's staring out of the window. I realise she hasn't yet met my eyes.

I tap her on the leg. "Are you OK?"

She smiles weakly at me. "Yeah, I'm fine. We'll talk tomorrow, OK?"

I nod. I feel worried. It's not like Maddy at all.

The shop is quiet the next morning, so Bob's showing me how to make these amazing handmade truffles. I get a text message from Maddy: 'Free 4 lunch? Need to tlk urgent.'

I send one back saying yes, of course. I feel relieved. I was worried she wasn't going to say anything to me about what happened with Leo, and I wouldn't have been at all comfortable not talking to her about it.

Bob's made a few dozen chocolates and I've eaten a good share of them by the time Maddy turns up. She doesn't look like herself at all. She's not wearing any make-up and she hasn't even straightened her hair. Things must be bad – she straightened her hair when she went into hospital to have her wisdom teeth out.

"Can we go out?" she asks.

I turn to Bob and he waves at the door. "Go. Go. Have a good one."

Maddy and I walk through the square, cross Traynor Lane and sit down on a bench in the Cathedral Gardens. It's another roasting hot day and we only managed to get a bench because Maddy gets an early lunch. In another half an hour, the entire square will be full of people with their shirts open and their trousers rolled up, trying to get a tan.

"So?" I say. "What's so urgent?"

Maddy turns and looks at me seriously. So seriously that my stomach flutters a little.

"I'm so, so sorry about this. I don't know where it came from and I so wish I did."

That's not what I'm expecting her to say at all, and I probably look confused. She takes a piece of paper out of her pocket, unfolds it and smooths it against her leg. And that's when I realise what it is.

It's a page from my diary.

"Where did you get it?" I ask. As I reach for it, I see that my hands are shaking.

"It was in my pocket last night. I nearly didn't notice it – it would have gone in the wash – but it was sticking out a bit. I guess whoever put it there didn't want to spend too much time pushing it right down inside."

"So someone at the party?"

Maddy nods. "I'm so sorry, Del."

I smooth the page with my hand. It's funny, the paper feels so familiar. The diary was a silk patterned covered one that I got in Chinatown in Manchester when a bunch of us went for Chinese New Year. The paper is slightly shiny, but rough around the edges. It was lovely to write on. It made my writing look much nicer than it actually is. The page has clearly been torn out of the book either in a hurry or without much care.

I read it and I'm relieved to see it's not quite as embarrassing as the last one. Well, it's all relative, of course, but at least I'm not talking about masturbation.

No, on this page I've written about how much I fancy Leo.

And how envious I am of Maddy for getting to spend so much time with him.

And how I wish he was my boyfriend.

Yes, I've actually written, 'I wish he was my boyfriend'. I don't know. I didn't give it a second thought when I wrote it in my diary, but seeing it there now, out of context, it just sounds pathetic and needy. It sounds like something an eight-year-old would write about, like Troy from *High School Musical*. I feel my cheeks getting hot. Again.

It's not even a recent entry. It was a while ago when I decided I'd wasted enough time on Dan and should, you know, move on to someone equally unobtainable (since he's into Maddy and not me, but I didn't know that then).

"Well, that's not at all embarrassing," I say. I scrunch the paper up and throw it in the nearest bin.

"What are you doing?!" Maddy says. She sounds horrified and she leaps to her feet.

"What?"

"That's evidence!" She sticks her hand in the bin

and, with her face scrunched up in horror, roots around until she finds the page. She pulls it out, folds it up, puts it back in her pocket and wipes her hands on her trousers.

"Evidence for what?" I ask. "Diary theft?"

"No! Blackmail."

"But don't you usually have to, you know, pay money or something? If someone's blackmailing you, I mean?"

"Well they still might..."

"Oh, well, that's something to look forward to."

"But even if it's not blackmail, it's certainly harassment and that's illegal too, you know!"

"Yeah, OK."

"And don't delete any emails or IMs or anything. You never know what could be important."

"OK."

"Promise?"

"I promise. Don't get so worked up."

She pulls a face. "I just hate to see this happening to you. And I wish I knew who was doing it."

"Me too," I say.

"Who was there last night, who was also at

Jamie's party?" she asks.

I frown. "Practically everyone."

"Oh, yeah. Right."

I lean back on the bench and close my eyes. It's so hot. The sun shines orange through my eyelids and it feels so good. I'm still tired from last night, but the sun's helping. We talk about the party and who hooked up with who, but Maddy doesn't mention what happened with her and Leo. I don't know whether to ask. But she's bound to tell me. We're best friends.

"OK," she says, standing up. "I'd better get back."

Oh. So she's not going to mention it? I can't quite believe it. Maybe she's going to come round later.

"Can you come round later?" I ask.

"No, sorry. Going out with Sid."

"Anywhere good?"

"Probably not. Maybe just the cinema."

"Right."

"You seeing Dan?"

"Not sure. He said he'd ring, but he hasn't yet."

"OK. I'll give you a ring in the morning then." She hugs me and says, "I'm so sorry about the diary."

"I know. Thanks for telling me about it."

Maddy heads off briskly down the hill, while I trudge back to the deli. I can't believe she didn't mention what happened with Leo last night. We've never had secrets before. At least, as far as I know. I suppose if she did have secrets, I wouldn't know them, would I? Because they are secret. Still. I'm surprised. It's such a massive thing – getting off with Leo! If she doesn't mention it, I don't know how long I'll be able to stay quiet.

I cross the road at the zebra crossing.

It's ridiculous. I mean, what's she going to do? Is she going to finish with Sid? It doesn't sound like it since she's going out with him tonight. Is she planning to keep seeing both of them? How would that work? I just can't get my head around any of it.

I walk up the square towards the deli and see Dan standing outside, presumably waiting for me. I feel my face break into a smile and I see him smile back. He's got a great smile.

As I get closer, he takes a few steps towards me and wraps his arms around me. I hug him around his waist and feel him kiss the place where my neck meets my shoulder. It feels lovely.

"You OK?" he asks, stepping back.

"Yeah, thanks. Tired..."

"Yeah, me too."

He pushes me gently up against the wall of the bridal shop next to the deli and kisses me. I push him away just as gently and say, "I'm really sorry, I've got to get back to work."

"I thought we could go somewhere for lunch."

"I'm sorry. I've just had my lunch break with Maddy."

"Oh right, cool. Did she tell you about her and Leo?"

"No."

"No?" He looks surprised.

"No, she came to tell me something else."

"Oh right. Is it weird that she didn't tell you about last night?"

"Yeah, it is," I say. "But I'm sure she will. Maybe she's still working it out herself."

"Yeah, probably."

"She brought me a page from my diary that someone put in her pocket last night."

"What?" He looks horrified. "Someone put a page from your diary in her pocket at the party?"

I nod.

"Shit. Who the hell would do that?"

"That's what I'd like to know."

"Shit."

"Yeah. I'm sorry, I'd better go." I kiss him again and he says he'll phone me this evening.

When I go back in the deli, Bob is serving a customer, but winks at me when I come in.

I take my coat off and then make myself a cup of coffee. Once the customer's gone, Bob says, "So things are going well with lover boy then?" He rolls his 'r's in 'loverrrrrrboy' and I laugh. "Yeah, it seems to be going well."

I still can't believe it, actually. It just seems a bit far-fetched that Dan Bailey is waiting for me outside the deli, pushing me up against the wall to kiss me, swearing at the idea of someone nicking my diary. I don't understand why I'm so insecure about it all. Why wouldn't he like me? I'm nice. I'm bright. I'm funny. Sometimes. I'm even quite pretty – according to Maddy, anyway. How come

Jamie got all the confidence and self-belief, and I got none? I think I'll have to think about that tomorrow. But then, if I'm going to think about that tomorrow, that means I'll have to think about Maddy and Leo today, and I don't really want to. Can I just think about everything tomorrow?

"Tomorrow never comes," Bob says, and I realise I've said the last part aloud. I cringe.

"So, how's Maddy?" Bob asks.

I start re-organising the spices again. Bob laughs at me for doing it so often, but they're always in a mess – do customers deliberately rearrange them? – but I don't care because I find it therapeutic.

"She's fine," I say.

"So did you find your diary?" he asks.

"Kind of," I say. His face gets redder and redder as I tell him (leaving out some of the more embarrassing details, obviously) and then he says "Have you called the police?"

"I don't think it's a police matter, is it?"

"I've never told you what happened to me, have I?" he says. He seems really agitated, marching up and down in front of the shop window.

I shake my head.

"Right, well, you know when I went travelling?"

"With your dad's credit card?" I ask, smiling a bit. I'm trying to lighten the mood and usually that detail does make Bob smirk, but it doesn't work this time. He just nods.

"Well, I kept a diary. It was an important part of it for me. I was trying to experience stuff. You know, live a little. We'd just read Kerouac's *On the Road* at school and it really meant something to me. That's what I wanted to do. I wanted to travel and write and—" He shakes his head quite violently, as if he's trying to clear it. "I mean, I didn't know at the time that that's what everyone wants to do when they read Kerouac. I didn't know I was such a cliché. I thought I'd found my life's purpose and all that. Anyway, I wrote all the time, and the others used to take the piss out of me, but I loved it. And then my diary went missing."

I feel my eyebrows shoot up and Bob stops pacing and looks at me. "I searched for it everywhere. I searched people's bags while they were asleep. By the time we got to Lisbon, no one was speaking to me, unsurprisingly. I thought I'd made friends I'd have for life, you know? But that ruined everything. Don't let it do the same to you, Del."

He's looking at me really intensely now. I don't think I've ever seen him like this before and I'm kind of transfixed.

"It's not about you," he says. "Don't let it make you embarrassed or ashamed or suspicious. It's not about your diary. It's not about you. It's about envy and bitterness and you mustn't let it change you."

"That's what Dan says," I manage to squeak out.

"Well, Dan sounds like a top bloke."

When I get home, I strip off and get in the shower and start thinking about Leo. No, not like that. I'm wondering what his deal is with Maddy. And then I think about the hideously embarrassing page from my diary. And then I think, someone put that specific page in Maddy's pocket. And that, last night, Leo and Maddy were all over each other. Could Leo have been the one to put that page in her pocket while they were kissing?

I go cold, even though the water is hot. He couldn't have, could he? Could Leo have taken my diary and, if so, why? I can't imagine it being him, but it does seem like a weird coincidence. And if he is seeing Gemima, maybe they've done it together. I know Dan said she wouldn't do it if she wasn't going to get any 'credit', but maybe they've cooked up a plan. Or maybe I'm just paranoid. Never mind thinking about it tomorrow, I really wish I didn't have to think about any of this at all. It's doing my head in.

On Friday night, Dan rings and suggest that we go out for the day on Saturday. I did suggest I meet him at the station, but he insisted on coming round. So, on Saturday morning he turns up at the house. My plan was to go straight out of the door, but Dan – not to mention my parents – have other ideas. Mum is right behind me when I let Dan in and she ushers him straight into the kitchen. The two of them start chatting immediately and I feel like a spare part. Great.

I'm about to follow them into the kitchen when my dad thunders down the stairs, pushes past me and eagerly introduces himself to Dan. He shakes his hand forcefully – I know from him doing it to Jamie's boyfriends that he does it on purpose as a test. But I think Dan must have passed because Dad turns to me and winks.

Minutes later, the four of us are sitting at the table, with Mum pouring coffee and Dad trying to interest us in croissants.

"So where are you off to today?" Dad asks Dan.

"We thought we'd go up to Lytham St Annes," Dan says.

It was actually Dan's idea to go to Lytham, and at first it completely freaked me out. After Jamie's party, I remember fantasising about maybe spending the summer with Dan and going up to Lytham for the day, and I can't quite believe it's coming true.

"I used to take Del's mum up to Lytham for dirty weekends," Dad says. He's trying to embarrass Dan, but Dan just laughs.

"We'll just be having good clean fun," he says, smiling at me.

I was hoping we could get going, but Dan's

buttering a croissant, so we're stuck here for a while. "What time's the train?" I ask.

Dan shrugs. "They're every half hour, don't worry."

Dad asks Dan if he's thought about what he wants to do for a career – God, he's embarrassing – and, as Dan starts talking about graphic design, my mobile buzzes.

It's Maddy: What u doing 2day?

I reply: Me and D going to Lytham

Maddy: Cool.

Me: U ok?

My phone rings and I step out of the kitchen to answer it. It's Maddy.

"Would you mind if we came to Lytham too?" she asks immediately.

"No, I don't think so. Why?"

"I don't know. Things are a bit weird between us and I think a day at the seaside would do us good."

"Between you and Sid?" I ask, even though I know things are probably weird with Leo too.

"Yeah," she says. "I just feel like we need a bit of a change."

"Yeah, that's fine. I don't know what train we're getting, but it'll probably be in the next hour or so."

"Oh right, I thought you'd be on your way."

"No. Dan's having breakfast with my parents."

"Oh, Jesus!" she says and laughs. "Things must be serious."

I hear loud laughter from the kitchen. "Well, they're laughing, so it must be going OK."

"Your parents are great," Maddy says. "He'll love them."

"Yeah, but if he spends the rest of the day telling me how gorgeous my mum is, I'll stab him with a candyfloss stick."

Maddy laughs. "You're mad. It's you he thinks is gorgeous, not your mum!"

We arrange to ring or text when we get to Lytham, and I go back to the kitchen.

An hour or so later we're finally at the station. I text Maddy to let her know and she replies that they're already on an earlier train.

Before we get our train, Dan buys a coffee and

I get a smoothie. It's already a hot day and the forecast says it's going to be in the eighties in the afternoon. Lytham's probably going to be heaving, but it'll be great to go on the beach.

The train is packed – and smells of suncream – but we manage to get two seats and, once we're sitting down, Dan kisses me.

"I love your parents," he says.

I scrunch my face up. "Kissing me made you think of my parents?"

He laughs. "No, I'm just saying. They're really funny and cool."

"Yeah. If you don't have to live with them."

"You get on with them, don't you?"

"Yeah, I do. But my dad is embarrassing, and my mum..."

"Your mum's great!"

"Yeah, that's the problem. Everyone always goes on about how gorgeous my mum is. All my life people have been telling me how beautiful she is, and then they started saying it to Jamie too. Or saying how much Jamie is like Mum. And then there's me..."

"You're gorgeous too," Dan says and kisses me again. "You know you're gorgeous, don't you?"

I don't really know how to answer that. I don't want to be all girlie and sound like I'm fishing for compliments, but do I know I'm gorgeous? No.

"Not really," I end up saying. "No."

"I think you are," he says and kisses me from my shoulder up to my neck, along my jaw and then back to my lips. It makes me melt and, for a second, I do feel gorgeous.

We pretty much spend the rest of the journey kissing. By the time we get to Lytham, my head is spinning and I barely know where I am. Honestly, I can't bear to think about all the years I wasted not kissing. Why didn't anyone tell me?

I don't know if it's all the kissing or what, but when we get to Lytham, I'm absolutely starving. Holding hands, me and Dan walk down to the prom where I immediately smell chips. Is there anything better than the smell of chips when you're hungry? Once I smell them, I feel almost desperate to get some; if the chippy was closed, I'd smash the window and cook them myself.

"If I don't get some chips, someone's going to get hurt," I growl and Dan laughs, speeding up and pulling me along with him.

"It's a chip emergency!"

"It's OK for you," I say as we cross the car park towards the pier and – importantly – the chip shop. "You had breakfast with my parents. I was too nervous to eat this morning."

"Nervous about what?" Dan says. He almost bangs his head on a canoe sticking out from a roof rack on a Nissan Micra.

"They could have someone's eye out with that," he says.

I grin at him and say, "About you coming to the house: I was hoping to just push you out and avoid Mum and Dad, but oh no..."

He laughs. "Why? I don't know why you didn't want me to meet them. They're great."

"I know," I say. "And so are you." I squeeze his hand. "I hope you'll all be very happy together."

He laughs again and, pulling me tight against him, kisses me hard.

"Hey!" I say, pretending to be outraged. "No time for that. Chips!"

"Oh, right, chips." He keeps his arm wrapped around me as we go into the chip shop and join the queue.

I can hear Sid's voice, so I lean out of the queue and see Maddy, Sid and Leo at the front getting their own chips. I can't quite believe it's the three of them. How's that going to work? I was sure Maddy planned this trip to be for her and Sid. What's Leo doing here, as well?

"It's Mads, Sid and Leo," I whisper to Dan and his eyebrows shoot up. So it's not just me – he thinks it's weird too.

I lean out of the queue again and call Maddy's name. Spotting me, she grins and comes over. She gives me a quick hug and says hello to Dan.

"We were starving when we got here!" she says.

"Me too," I say, weakly. I feel a bit shaky and I'm not sure why. Is it just because Maddy's behaving so out of character? Or maybe I'm just starving.

"It's the fresh sea air," Dan says.

Maddy laughs. "I don't think we've had any yet,

we came straight here."

Sid and Leo walk past with their chips and nod and smile at me and Dan. Maddy says they'll wait for us outside. Dan and I stand in silence until we get to the front of the queue where I finally get my chips. I feel so hungry, I could just rip the paper open and start scoffing them before we've even paid – but I manage to contain myself.

Outside, Maddy, Sid and Leo are sitting on bollards and are already digging into their chips.

The five of us walk down the slipway to the beach and then sit on the low wall that runs under the pier. I tilt my face up to the sun again and then tear open my chips.

Dan pinches one immediately and I say, "Hey! Watch it. I'll have your hand off."

The first chip is always the best and, as I put it in my mouth, I think: I'm here, at the beach, with my friends and my...boyfriend (I'm not quite comfortable with that word yet), sitting in the sun and eating chips. Things must be good, right? Famous last words.

15

Once we've all finished stuffing our faces, we wander along the beach towards the boating lake. The beach is pretty chocka, with families flying kites and crowds of lads playing football. Sid and Leo run down to the water's edge, but Dan stays with me and Maddy, holding my hand.

"So are things OK then?" I ask Maddy. I doubt she'll say anything in front of Dan, but you never know.

"Yeah, they're fine," she says.

"Things OK with you and Sid?"

"Yeah," she says again. She looks out towards

the sea where Sid and Leo are pushing each other towards the water.

"They're like kids, aren't they?" I say, smiling.

"More like Labradors, I always think," she says.

We climb up the steps to the boating lake and then, knackered from the heat, flake out on the grass. Sid and Leo run up and shake water all over us.

"See?" Maddy says. "Labradors."

We lie there for a few minutes, just soaking up the sun. I get bored really easily just lying about in the sun, and I don't tan, so I prop myself up on my elbows and look at Dan. He's lying down with his eyes closed and he looks gorgeous.

Seeing him lying next to me, makes me think about lying next to him in bed and I immediately feel myself blush. And then I have a sudden panic. Should I be sleeping with him by now? We've only actually been out a couple of times, but I don't know what boys expect. We've only kissed, we haven't even done any touching. Well, a bit. But only over clothes.

I need to talk to Maddy about it. I need to talk to Maddy about a lot of things. I'll have to make sure she comes round to mine or I go to hers with no boyfriends – or Leo, whatever he is these days – around so we can really talk.

I'm still staring at Dan when he opens his eyes and grins at me, squinting because of the sun. "What are you thinking about?" he asks.

"You," I say. I lean over and kiss him and he rolls on top of me. I scream.

Maddy laughs. "Get a room."

I hear Dan say something that sounds like "Oof!" and then he rolls off me, rubbing the back of his head. I sit up and realise that Sid or Leo has belted a football into the back of Dan's head. Oh, great, football. Dan jumps up and the three of them are off.

I don't know what gets into boys where football is concerned. Within seconds, it's like they're in another world. Shouting incomprehensible stuff to each other and running around like nutters, kicking the ball, thinking they're 'it'. It's weird. Is there anything that makes girls behave like that?

Maddy sits up next to me and I ask, again, "Are you OK?"

Maddy sighs. "No." She reaches into her bag and takes out a pack of cigarettes.

"I didn't think so," I say, glancing at the cigs. She's definitely smoking more.

"I don't really want to talk about it yet," she says. "Is that OK?"

I'm surprised, but I nod.

"I will talk to you about it soon, it's just... I'm trying to work out what I want without anyone else's opinion."

I'm looking at her and trying to work out exactly what's going on, when I hear a splash and then laughter. I look over to see that one of the three boys has kicked the football into the boating lake.

"Dan, Dan, Dan!" Sid and Leo start chanting.

"I think it must have been Dan," Maddy says, smiling as she lights up a fag.

They run over towards the boating lake and me and Maddy get up and follow them. As he goes, Dan kicks off his trainers and pulls his T-shirt over his head.

"Hello!" Maddy says and I slap her, jokingly.

"Back off, he's mine."

"Nice bod," she says and I smile. He really has. He's a bit tanned and he's got some definition: pecs and nice shoulders.

I watch Dan as he tries to tiptoe around all the goose and duck poo. He finally makes it in and splashes about in the lake – messing around and pretending he can't get the ball – while Sid and Leo stand on the steps almost falling over with laughter.

"It doesn't take much, does it?" Maddy says.

I smile at her and then go back to watching Dan. His hair's wet and he looks amazing.

"So you haven't slept together or anything?" Maddy says, quietly.

I feel a flash of annoyance, which surprises me. Of course Maddy would ask me that. And of course I would tell her if anything had happened. But while she's keeping secrets from me, I really don't think she should be asking me anything like that.

"No," I say. "Not yet."

"Good," she says and I feel annoyed again.

"Why good?" I ask her. I can feel my face getting red.

"I just don't think you should rush into anything, you know?"

"No," I say. "I don't know. Why not?"

"Well, you know." She takes a massive drag on her cigarette and, at that moment, she just doesn't seem like my best friend at all. "He's your first boyfriend. You just don't want to do too much, too soon."

"Maybe I do," I say. I feel, suddenly, inexplicably furious. I mean, who is she to tell me what to do after what she's been doing? "Maybe that's exactly what I want to do! Maybe shagging Dan is exactly what I need! How would you know it's not?"

Maddy winces and, at the same time, I sense a change in the atmosphere. Yes, of course. The boys had stopped pissing about and were totally listening. As soon as I realise, I get that stomach-dropping feeling again. I'm getting it a lot lately. And I could really do without it. I'm almost afraid to look at Dan. I can see from Sid's face – which is kind of horrified, but, at the same time, I think a bit impressed – that this could go either way. So I force myself to look at Dan.

And his face? He looks like he's not sure whether

to laugh or to jump me. He looks...incredibly sexy. And I start to think that shagging Dan could well be exactly what I need to do.

We walk back along the prom while Dan dries off. He holds my hand and keeps laughing.

"What?" I say, more than once.

"You were just so cute! Shouting about shagging me. You know there was an old lady who keeled right off a bench?"

"There was not!"

"Yeah, there was. And a little kid dropped his ice cream."

"Shut up."

"And a seagull fell out of the sky. He was so shocked, he just forgot to flap his wings. It was sad, really."

I laugh. "You're not funny."

He wraps his arm around my shoulder and I try to push it away. "Ew! You're still wet!"

He shakes his wet hair at me and I try to pull away again, but he's not having it. He pulls me back and kisses me.

"I'm so embarrassed," I say.

"Don't be," Dan says. "It's one of the things I like most about you."

"What is?" I'm not fishing; I'm genuinely confused.

"How you just say what's on your mind."

"Me?" I say. I can't believe it. That's one of the last things I'd say about myself. "I don't," I say.

"Yeah, you do. You've said loads of stuff to me that must have been hard to say."

"Like what?" Honestly, I'm amazed. My parents and Jamie are the ones who say what's on their mind in my family. I'm always too worried about what people think of me.

"You asked me about Gemima. You asked why I asked you out. You told the whole of Lytham you want to shag me..."

I shove him again, but he just kisses me again. "You just say when," he says.

I laugh. "I don't know about that."

"Oh," he says. "I was just joking. You don't need to worry. I just wanted you to know that when you're ready, I'm ready."

I actually stop walking, I'm so surprised. "Really?"

He grins. "Yes, really."

I say quietly, "You'd want to?"

He makes his voice deep and low and says, "Oh, yeeaah." And I laugh.

"OK," I say. "I'll bear that in mind."

He hugs me again and I don't even mind that he's still sopping wet. And now so am I.

16

Back at the pier, we get ice creams and then go into the arcade. Me and Dan play air-hockey, and then the five of us have a go at the tenpin bowling.

I can't help watching Maddy with Sid and Leo. And Sid and Leo together. They all seem like their normal selves. There's certainly no tension between Sid and Leo, and I don't really notice anything between Maddy and Leo either. I do occasionally see her looking at him, perhaps more than she would have looked at him before. But maybe not... I mean, we've always agreed he was gorgeous, and maybe we always looked at him. I don't know.

Once we've exhausted all the penny falls and the other crappy machines (like that one where you press the button like a nutter to make a horse run), we start walking back to the station.

I feel different. Dan is holding my hand and playing with my fingers and stroking my wrist and I'm thinking 'boyfriend' and I feel OK about it. In fact, I feel good about it.

We get on the train together and Sid falls asleep pretty much immediately. And that's when I notice a difference with Leo and Maddy. They're sitting opposite each other and just...staring at each other.

Dan clearly notices too, because he starts making really obvious small-talk about people at school, teachers, his parents (I listen carefully to that bit, because he hasn't really mentioned his parents to me before: his mum's a psychotherapist and his dad works as a drugs counsellor). Maddy and Leo aren't being really obvious about not listening, but you can tell they're not.

After a while Dan starts saying more and more outrageous stuff. About his sister, Rose Marie, who's a trapeze artist with the Moscow State Circus.

And his dog, Sniffer, who was kidnapped by local radio DJs. And Maddy and Leo don't even notice. Dan grins at me, and I grin back, but I still can't help wondering – and worrying – about Maddy.

We all sit in silence for a while, my head on Dan's shoulder. Sun and sea air really does make you sleepy. We're just approaching Preston train station when Dan's mobile buzzes with a text. He reads it and looks puzzled.

"Something wrong?" I ask.

He shakes his head. "Something weird. I think this was really meant for you." He holds the phone out to me and, on the small display I see these words:

Sometimes when I touch myself, I think about Sawyer from Lost. Sometimes I think about Dan.

Oddly, my first thought is, "For God's sake!". For once I'm not blushing, I don't know why. I do feel embarrassed, but I also feel pissed off. Pissed off that whoever is doing this has ruined a really cool day. Pissed off that they've gone to so much trouble to try and embarrass me in front of Dan. Dan's not looking at me now, he's pressed a button and he's got the phone up to his ear.

"Switched off," he says and then smiles at me. "Sawyer? Really?"

"He's sexy," I say.

Dan holds the phone up. "That was sexy."

Now I start to blush. "What?"

"You touch yourself and think about me? Are you kidding? That's beyond sexy!"

I put my hands up to my now red-hot cheeks and find myself covering my face. "Really?"

He pulls my hands down. "Really. And after that conversation we had earlier? Grrrooowwl!"

I laugh.

Dan kisses me and says, "Honestly. I wouldn't worry about it."

"What? That someone's deliberately harassing me with my own embarrassing diary?"

"Yes! They're your thoughts, right? It's not something someone's made up about you."

"Well, yeah. But they're my private thoughts. Or, at least, they're supposed to be private."

"But so what?" I pull a face and he laughs. "No,

I mean, so what if they're not private anymore. Are you ashamed of what you wrote?"

"Little bit," I say.

He squeezes me to him. "But are you? Or are you just ashamed now that other people are reading it?"

I shake my head. I see what he's getting at, but it's not his private thoughts and feelings that are being spewed all over town.

"You know," he says. "You should never be ashamed of the truth."

"But could you?" I ask him. "Could you be all out and proud having people read all your private stuff? Whether it's the truth or not?"

"First of all," he says. "I don't know what you're implying by 'out and proud', but I thought I'd made it quite clear to you—"

I laugh and give him a shove. "You know what I mean!"

"And secondly, yeah, my private thoughts are between me and my privates, as some old comedian once said. But if they were out there in the world – my private thoughts, I mean, not my privates – I'd like to think I'd be OK with it."

"Really?" I say and he nods. "I don't believe you."

He laughs. "Well, I don't know, do I? But what I mean is, you can fight against it, and be devastated and ashamed and embarrassed, or you can just say, yeah, whatever, it's my diary, you shouldn't be reading it... Piss off."

"Poetry," I say, laughing.

"It's like that girl," he says. "What was that girl who got expelled for that fingering incident?"

"Alison Stevens," I say.

"Well, she didn't apologise or grovel, she just said it's a fair cop and off she went. It was on her MySpace wasn't it? I thought she was going to go on *X Factor* or something and be all, 'The thing is, Simon, I got expelled for getting fingered...' You know. Run with it. Make it your USP."

"You want me to make the fact that my diary is being read by who-knows-who my unique selling point?"

He grins. "Why not?"

"You're mad."

"Sexy mad?" He waggles his eyebrows and I laugh.

"No. Just mad."

"OK, put it this way. You'll be notorious. Everyone will know you."

"I don't want everyone to know me."

"Really? You don't want to be famous?"

I laugh. "No!"

"You could probably get a topless spread in *Nuts* on the back of it..."

"No!"

"OK. I can't pretend to understand it, but I respect it."

I roll my eyes.

"So you don't want to be famous, you don't want to be a glamour model. You don't want to go on *The X Factor*?"

"No!"

"OK. Weird." He grins. "So what do you want?"

"I just want to be left alone."

"But do you? Do you really? People say that, but they don't really mean it. You've got good friends. You've got a great family. You've got me." He waggles his eyebrows again. "You don't want to be left alone."

"OK, no." I sigh and look over at Maddy and Leo.

Leo's looking out of the window and Maddy looks like she's texting. They both seem like they're in their own worlds and they're certainly not listening to me and Dan.

"So what you want is for people not to know your private thoughts and feelings?"

I sigh again. "God. I don't know."

He laughs. "You want people to know your private thoughts and feelings?"

"I want people to know the stuff I want them to know. Everything else I want to keep private."

"But how does that work?"

"I don't know."

"People are always going to know things about you you'd prefer they didn't know."

"OK, you tell me something. Tell me something private about you. Tell me something you'd be embarrassed to have read out in assembly."

He snorts. "OK." He sits for a minute, thinking. I can tell he's thinking, because he's rubbing his chin and scrunching his eyes up.

"Stop taking the piss," I say. "Just tell me something."

"OK. I bought McFly's 'All About You'. Not because it was for charity, but because I liked it."

"Pssshhhh!" I say.

He grins. "Right. I took my nephews to see *WALL-E* at the cinema and I cried."

I shake my head.

"I cried and they didn't!"

I keep shaking my head.

"They're four and six!"

I'm still shaking my head.

"OK, OK. In Year 8, I was sick in the dining hall..."

"That's not embarrassing!"

"Let me finish!"

"I was sick in the dining hall and Mrs Sherwood took me to see the nurse. On the way, she held my hand and, by the time we got there, I had a hard-on."

I cover my mouth with my hands. "No!"

He grins. "Yes!"

Mrs Sherwood was our dinner lady. No-one knew her exact age, but guesses ranged from sixty to ninety.

"Wow," I say. "Was it just that one time or did you fall for her?"

He laughs. "It was just that one time. I mean, to be fair, that year pretty much anything could give me an erection. The sun coming out. Sitting down. Standing up. Those sexy Bunsen burners, all hot and shimmery..."

I laugh.

"Remember Mrs Kinnear?"

Mrs Kinnear was our deputy head for a year. She was awful. I nod.

"I remember one day sitting in assembly and looking over and she was wearing tights and she had massively hairy legs. The hair was all matted under her tights and I couldn't stop staring. And then I couldn't stand up. I had to pretend I had cramp until things..." – he gestures at his crotch – "...went back to normal."

"Oh my God."

He passes me his phone. "Do you want to text that story back to whoever sent this one?"

I laugh, shaking my head. "No. I'm too embarrassed. I don't want people to know my boyfriend got the horn for Mrs Kinnear's hairy legs!"

"I'll do it," he says.

"I believe you," I say, laughing. "But there's no need. You've made your point."

"And do you get it?"

"Yeah, I get it. But I can't say I'm completely convinced."

"OK. I'll keep trying. I'll break you eventually," he says and kisses me again. As he's kissing me, I find myself thinking – well, as far as I *can* think when Dan's kissing me – maybe he's right. Maybe this isn't the worst thing that's ever happened. Maybe I should just say, "Yeah? So what?"

Dan pulls away and says, "Sorry. I was just thinking. Did you just call me your boyfriend?"

I blush. Again. "Yeah. I'm sorry, I—"

"Don't apologise," he says. "Boyfriend. I like it."

He kisses me again and this time I'm not thinking at all.

When we get off the train, Dan, Sid and Leo go off to get their buses and me and Maddy start walking.

"You and Dan seemed very cosy," she says.

I smile. "Yeah. He's lovely."

"He is. He's great," she says. "Are you doing anything tonight?"

I shake my head.

"Is it OK if I come round?"

"Of course."

"I could stay the night, if you like."

I nod. "That sounds great."

This doesn't sound like Maddy at all. Usually

she'd just invite herself. She doesn't ask, she just does. This new Maddy makes me nervous.

When we get to Gillies Street, Maddy turns off and I carry on walking home. When I get in, Mum and Dad are lying out, sunbathing, in the garden. Mum's in a bikini and Dad's wearing shorts with monkeys printed on them. And they wonder why I don't like bringing my friends home.

I get them each a cold beer from the fridge and join them in the garden. They sit up on the ground and I sit down on the garden swing.

"Good day?" Mum asks.

"Good day to you, sir," I say. It's a family joke. Well, I say 'joke'... "Yeah, it was great," I add. "It's OK if Maddy stays the night tonight, isn't it?"

"Great, yeah," Dad says. "We could watch *Shaun of the Dead* and...what goes with zombies? Nachos?"

My dad always wants to have theme evenings. It probably seems a bit weird hanging out with your friends and your parents, but mine can actually be quite a good laugh. Not tonight, though. That's not what tonight's about.

"I don't think so," I say.

"Spaghetti?" Dad says. "'Cos of that bit with Dylan Moran when they pull his guts out..."

"Lovely," I say. "But I mean it, no. No theme evening. Me and Maddy need to talk."

"Boy problems?" Dad says, putting his head on one side.

"No. Nothing like that," I say. "We just haven't had a chance to talk for a little while and we need to catch up."

"Oh yeah. You need to tell her all about Dan. What you've done. What you haven't done. What you think you should've done..."

I cover my ears with my hands. "Dad! Stop!"

"At this point," my mum says. "I should probably ask you what you've done and, you know, whether you were safe..."

"Mum! Don't you start. We haven't done anything we'd need to be safe for!" I say.

"Yet," she says. "But you will."

I think of my conversation with Dan earlier and my mum obviously sees it on my face because she says, "Just make sure, when the time comes, you, you know, do what you need to do."

"Right," I say. "Thanks."

"You do know what you need to do, don't you?" my Dad says and I cringe again.

"Yes, I know. Thank you."

"Because your grandad said he knew what to do and..." He holds his arms wide. "Here I am!"

"Dad," I say. "I know what to do."

"OK."

I start to get up and my dad pinches my knee. "And if you need, you know, anything, your sister's got a ton of them in her bedside drawer."

When Maddy arrives, we go straight up to my room.

"My dad fancied a *Shaun of the Dead* evening tonight," I say.

"Ooh," she says. "What goes with *Shaun of the Dead*? Pizza!"

"Ugh," I say. "I'd never be able to eat pizza again. Anyway, I told him no."

"Why?" She starts piling all the cushions from around the floor of my room onto the bed.

"'Cos we need to talk. Don't we?"

She arranges the cushions and my pillows and

sits with her back to the headboard. "Yeah, we do."

"OK," I say. I pull my beanbag up against the wall and slump down.

"I slept with Leo," Maddy says.

"Jesus Christ!" I say. "Break it to me gently, why don't you?"

She smiles. "Sorry. I've been trying to think of the best way to say it and I decided...just come out with it."

"Shit." I've actually got butterflies in my stomach. I feel like I've had a proper fright. I don't know what to say.

"Sorry," she says again. "It's just really hard for me to talk about – you might have noticed." She looks down at me and smiles weakly.

"Yeah," I say. "You haven't exactly been yourself."

"No. OK, so you know I've been thinking about Leo?"

I nod.

"Well, I sort of told him."

"You told him you fancied him?"

"I told him I thought I might be in love with him."

"Oh my God."

"I know. But I couldn't help it. It just came out. We were round at Sid's and his mum was freaking out because he'd put a tea-towel in the wrong drawer or something."

Sid's mum is really particular. Like, OCD particular.

"So he was downstairs dealing with that," Maddy continues. "And he'd been gone a while and there was this atmosphere between me and Leo. At least, I thought there was. And it just got worse and worse until it was all I could think about and then it just burst out of me."

"That you love him?" I can't believe it. I can't believe anyone could be so brave. Or possibly mad. It's hard to say.

"No. Well, yes. But first I said that I couldn't stop thinking about him and I knew it was wrong because he's Sid's best friend, but I had to tell him."

"And what did he say?" I didn't even notice that I'd moved, but I'm now kneeling on the beanbag and leaning on the bed, like a meerkat.

"Well first of all he looked absolutely terrified.

197

Like, really. Like he was going to cry or throw up or something. I think I probably looked the same, though. I definitely felt the same. And then he said that it was ridiculous and Sid was his best mate and, never mind Sid, I was one of his best mates and he couldn't believe I was saying this."

"Right..." I say.

There's a knock at my door and my dad sticks his head round. "We're ordering food. What do you fancy?"

"Pizza?" Maddy asks and my dad says, "Pizza it is!" and disappears again.

I don't really fancy pizza, particularly now Maddy's made me associate it with zombies, but no one asked me, did they?

"So, then what?" I ask Maddy.

"Well, I started thinking that Sid wouldn't be much longer and so I didn't say anything else. And then, a couple of minutes later, Sid came back up and that was that."

"And when was this?"

"The night before Cobby's party," she says.

Oh yes. Cobby's party. I haven't decided yet

whether to admit to having seen her and Leo at the party. On the one hand, I think if she's telling me anyway, then I might as well say I saw them, but then, on the other hand, it would mean me admitting that I knew about it, but didn't say anything. But she didn't say anything either. I don't know.

"So at the party, Sid had wandered off somewhere – the pool I think – and so me and Leo were outside and... Well, I don't know quite what happened – we weren't even talking – but we kind of ended up halfway down the garden and then... we kissed."

I try to do a surprised face, but it's obviously not that convincing because she frowns and says, "Who told you?"

I drop my head onto the bed and say, "We saw you."

"Who?"

I lift my head up again. "Me and Dan. We were at the bottom of the garden, by the river."

"Ah, on the bench? Yeah, we did notice there were people on the bench. Eventually. I didn't realise it was you and Dan."

"Sorry," I say. "I was going to say something, but then when you didn't... I didn't know what to do."

"No, I should have told you before now," she says. "But I've been freaking out about it all."

"I'm not surprised. So then...what?"

"We talked on the phone. And...I don't know. He's amazing. He's so funny and sweet and...sexy."

"And Sid?"

"Yeah, I know. I mean, I love Sid. I do. I know it seems ridiculous because basically I'm two-timing him, but I don't want to hurt him."

"This is going to hurt him," I say.

"I know. But I was thinking, would it be so wrong to see both of them?"

I laugh. "How is that going to work?"

She shakes her head. "I don't know, but it's worth a try, isn't it? I mean, why do I have to choose?"

"You just do," I say.

"I don't know. I mean, a threesome is every boy's dream, isn't it?"

I laugh again. "Yeah, with two girls!"

We're quiet for a while and then Maddy says, "Del, I'm sorry about what I said in Lytham."

"That's OK," I say. "I know you're just being overprotective, but I'm not one of your sisters."

"No, I know. But you're not really going to sleep with Dan, are you?"

"No," I say. "Not yet."

We end up watching *Shaun of the Dead* after all and, after the film, me and Maddy go back upstairs to get ready for bed. Once the lights are out, I say, "You didn't tell me about sleeping with Leo."

"Right," Maddy says. "It was weird. I mean, it was good, but it was still weird for it just to be us two. You know, I'm so used to the three of us hanging out, it was weird even to be on my own with Leo."

"Especially when you got naked, I imagine," I say.

Maddy laughs. "Actually, no. That was quite easy."

"Piss off," I say. "How could it be easy?"

"It just was. It was harder for us to have a conversation than to, you know..."

"So how was it?"

"The sex?" She whispers the word 'sex'. "It was really, really good. Exactly what I was talking about.

You know, when I said about how it had got so boring with Sid?"

I nod. Even though we're in the dark and she can't see me.

"Well, it was nothing like being with Sid. It was exciting. So, you and Dan...?"

"Haven't done anything yet. But it's going to happen. Soon, I think."

"How do you know?"

I tell her about the text and the conversation with Dan.

"He's right," she says.

"I know," I say. "I think. Well, I agree in theory, it's just hard, isn't it? It's hard not to be embarrassed at, you know, dirty laundry."

"Oh, God, I know. I mean, I wouldn't want people to find out about me and Leo, obviously. But it's nobody's business."

It's dark, so I feel like I can say stuff I wouldn't normally say. "But masturbation's always embarrassing, isn't it?"

She laughs. "Well, not for boys. I mean, think about it. They call each other wanker and tosser.

They say stuff about rubbing one out and having one off the wrist and all that. But girls just don't talk about it really."

"No..." I say, vaguely. It's one of those situations where I don't want to say too much in case it's just me. Do you know what I mean? Like, I could say "Oh yes, because I do it every day" (I don't really) and then Maddy would say, "Every day! Oh my God, you freak!" So I'm sticking with vagueness.

"But we all do it."

"Really?" I say.

"What?" she says. "Yeah, didn't you know that? I mean, I don't know for a fact, but I'm fairly sure."

"You do it?" I ask. And, even though it's dark and therefore less embarrassing, I still close my eyes tight when I say it.

"Of course! Didn't your mum ever talk to you about it?"

I laugh. "No!"

"I'm really surprised. I would have thought that was the kind of thing your mum would want to tell you all about. Or even your dad."

We both laugh and I say, "Ew. Can you imagine?"

"What about Jamie?"

"What about Jamie?" I say.

"Did she never say anything to you about it?"

"No. She doesn't talk to me about anything like that. Thank God. So what did your mum say?"

"Oh, God, it was painful. I mean, I'm glad she told me about it. I mean, I'm glad she didn't just do the 'when a man and a woman love each other they have a special hug' thing. You know, she talked about everything in great detail. Too much detail, to be honest. Didn't need to know about the Ann Summers parties she's been to. Really didn't need to know how good Jim is at sex."

Jim's her stepdad. "I didn't need to know that either, thanks."

She laughs again. "I know. Have you ever heard your parents having sex?"

I scrunch my eyes up again. "Unfortunately, yes."

"Me too. It woke me up. I thought it was the radiators."

I snort with laughter. "I can remember when I was little trying to go into their bedroom and they'd put a latch on the door and they were saying, 'Just hang on a minute. Just come back in a minute' and I couldn't understand why. 'Why can't I come in? What are you doing?' So embarrassing!"

"See, it's not embarrassing," Maddy says. "You weren't to know. You were only little."

"I know. I wasn't embarrassed at the time! I'm embarrassed now!"

"Knowing you, you were embarrassed then."

I laugh. "Yeah, I wouldn't be surprised. Oh, and there was another time on holiday when me and Jamie came back in the afternoon and they were, you know, having a bit."

"Did you see them?"

"No, but we heard them. God, I'd blanked that out! They were embarrassed. Actually, no, Mum was, but Dad wasn't."

Maddy laughs. "I bet. I love your dad."

"Yeah, yeah."

"What about Jamie? You ever heard her?"

"No," I say. "There was that time Dad caught Will – that guy she picked up in Sainsbury's – naked in the loo, but apart from that, nothing."

"When did she lose her virginity, do you think?"

"No idea. I mean, she's had boyfriends since she was about ten, but you never know who's doing what, do you?"

"No. Me and Leo started going out when we were eleven, but we didn't do anything until I was fourteen."

"Sid, you mean."

"What?"

"You said 'Me and Leo'."

"Did I? Shit. I'll have to be careful of that."

I lean up on my elbow and look in her direction, even though I can't see anything in the dark. "What are you going to do about Sid?"

"I don't know. I have to tell him something. God, I can't imagine it. The thing about Sid is he's so oblivious he makes it easy to cheat on him."

"That's not fair," I say.

"I know. I just mean that he hasn't noticed anything's going on. As far as I can tell."

"I know. I thought that at the bowling and in Lytham. But that doesn't mean he's oblivious. It just means he trusts you. And Leo."

"God. I know. I'm awful. But I don't feel awful. Is that really bad?"

"I don't know," I say. "I've only just got going with one boyfriend. I can't imagine how you'd deal with two."

"I'll let you know if I work it out."

I smile. "You're OK. I don't see it being a problem."

18

On Monday morning, I'm working in the deli – well, I say working, I'm mostly just standing there, thinking about Dan and waiting for a customer. Bob's in the kitchen making his award-winning chocolate torte – the smell is phenomenal. My mouth's watering and I'm not entirely sure if it's because of the smell or my thoughts about Dan.

I look up when the bell rings and Mum comes in. She's wearing a vest top, a short skirt, sandals and sunglasses, which she pushes up on her head as soon as she gets through the door. I know that sounds very mutton for a mum, but she looks great.

She still looks like a model, but she also looks like she's just thrown everything on without thinking about it. I didn't inherit this skill. At all. I'm envious.

Usually, when I'm working, Mum and Dad just leave me to get on with it. They know that I'm hoping to run the deli myself once I've left school, and they think hands-on experience is the best thing for me. Also, the deli's just not busy enough for more than one of us – along with Bob – to be here all day. Because Bob can manage on his own, I can pick and choose when I work.

"What are you doing here?" I ask her. But, you know, nicely.

"Just thought I'd come and see my lovely daughter," she says, pinching my cheek as I roll my eyes. "I've got some shopping to do, some stuff to pick up..."

"So you're not here to work?"

"I might have a look at the accounts if you make me a coffee." She puts her bag on the shelf at the window and boosts herself up onto a stool, crossing her long legs. Good grief. It's a good job Bob doesn't fancy her, because if he did, that chocolate torte would never get made. (Bob insists he doesn't fancy Mum – he says she's clearly gorgeous, but she's not his type. We don't know what his type is, since we've never seen him with a girlfriend. He says he's married to his job.)

I get the accounts book from the back and make Mum a cappuccino, while Bob goes out for a bit of a chat. I hope he remembers to keep his hands out of his hair.

When I take everything through, they're both laughing and Bob's got his hands in his pockets. I'm not sure the inside of his pockets is any more hygienic than his hair, but what can you do?

"She seems to be having a great time," Mum's saying and, because I'm self-absorbed, at first I think she's talking about me. And Dan. But she's not, she's talking about Jamie. "I think they work pretty hard during the day, but then play hard at night."

"Ugh!" I say, heading back behind the counter. "Don't say that! Work hard and play hard!" I shudder. "It's ridiculous."

"I didn't say it," Mum says. Her cheeks have gone

a bit pink, because Dad hates that expression, too, and if he'd been here, he'd be massively taking the piss out of her right now. "I just said that they work hard...and then they play hard."

"Oh yeah," I say, grinning. "That's completely different."

"Shut up, you," she says, but she can't resist a quick gnaw on her little fingernail, which I happen to know she only does when she's embarrassed. She turns back to Bob. "They all go out together at night. Have parties on the beach..."

"Sounds like *The O.C.*" Bob says. "Better make sure she's behaving herself!"

Mum laughs. "Oh, she'll be OK. She's just being eighteen. God knows, I..." She glances over at me and I smirk back at her. I'd love to know what Mum got up to when she was a model in London – well, I think I would – but there's no way she's ever going to tell me in any detail. She doesn't want to give me any ideas.

At lunchtime, Dan comes in to see me. We sit in the window with iced coffee (which I never thought I'd like, but I absolutely love) and a slice each of Bob's chocolate torte.

"I've got something for you," Dan says, before leaning over and kissing me. When he pulls away, I feel myself glance out of the window and have a tiny moment of embarrassment before catching myself and thinking, "Who cares if anyone's looking? Why can't I kiss my boyfriend whenever and wherever I like?" I like the feeling. (The not-being-embarrassed feeling, as opposed to the kissing-my-boyfriend feeling. Although I like that too, obviously.)

I'm not quite sure how to respond to Dan's mention of 'something for me'. Am I supposed to go all girlie and say, "What is it? What is it?" or just wait for him to give it to me. I decide to just wait. But I smile at him while I'm waiting.

He reaches into his pocket and takes out his mobile. I must admit, I'm confused. He's giving me his phone? He's going to show me something on it? Surely it's not another message from my diary? He made it sound like something good!

"Ring me," he says, eyes twinkling.

"Ring...you?" I say, brilliantly.

He just grins. "Yeah. Ring me."

I take my phone out of my tabard – that word never gets easier to say – pocket and press the speed-dial button for Dan. After a couple of seconds his phone starts to ring. Well, not ring, exactly – it starts to play McFly's 'All About You'. The 'real music' version. I burst out laughing.

"Is that just for when I ring?" I ask.

Dan has his eyes closed and he's swaying from side to side, clicking his fingers to the music. He opens one eye to look at me. "Nope. This is now my ringtone!" He closes the eye again and I stare at him.

"But that's going to be embarrassing!" I say.

"Well, duh!" he says, eyes still closed. "But I like the song and I choose to have it as my ringtone and not care what others think." He opens his eyes and looks right at me.

"Ah," I say. "It's a little lesson!"

He leans forward and kisses me. "Yup. I know that me having a McFly ringtone is nowhere near as embarrassing as what's been happening to you."

"Oh, I don't know," I laugh, thinking about his

phone going off at football practice, or whatever.

"But," Dan continues, "it's the little shit who's doing this – and it is a little shit, otherwise they'd be doing it openly – who should be embarrassed and ashamed. Not you."

I feel my eyes well with tears. I know he's right. I feel that he is. But I still don't exactly want to see my diary pages projected on, say, the town hall or anything.

"And, whenever you feel embarrassed, you can think about me, at football, singing along with McFly."

"You don't have to sing along with it," I say, laughing.

"Oh, but I do," he says. "It's so catchy."

"Do you want to come round tonight?" I ask him.

"To your house?"

I nod.

"Yeah, that sounds good. Will your parents be there?"

"More than likely," I say. "Is that OK? You could have dinner. Although I have to warn you, they might be having one of their disgusting film and food nights. Like *SAW* with barbecued ribs."

"That sounds good," he says. "In a horrifying way."

I lean over and kiss him. And I don't give a thought to who might be looking through the window.

My parents are quite ridiculously excited about Dan coming round for dinner. Dad's done his usual tidying thing of shoving everything away in cupboards. Mum calls it "hidying" and it drives her mad, not only because she can never find anything for weeks afterwards, but also because he hides everything that makes the house our home.

But Mum's not much better – she's opened pretty much every window in the house and emptied so much Toilet Duck down the loo that it's started to look like an overflowing chemical experiment.

"Will you two calm down?" I'm sitting at the

dining table, flicking through a magazine, while my dad is going through the fruit bowl checking for damaged apples. "He's coming for dinner. It's not an inspection."

Dad bounces an apple off his inner elbow, catches it behind his back and says, "Ta-da!" Then he sits at the table next to me. "It's just such a big day," he says and then pinches my cheeks while I frown at him. "You've never brought a boy home before."

"I brought him home on Saturday."

"No, I dragged him in while you tried to get away. Not the same thing at all. This time you've volunteered."

"And I'm already regretting it," I say.

"Get out of the way and let me set the table," Mum says.

"No!" I look from one to the other. "Not at the table! Too much pressure. We need to get a takeaway and watch a film."

"But then when would we ask him about his intentions?" Mum asks. Dad snorts with laughter.

"You're both very funny," I say. "But I can ring him now and we can go out instead." I stand up and head for the door, but Dad grabs me and hugs me. "We're just winding you up. Has he seen *The Happening*?"

"Oh God, we can't make him watch that," I say. "He might never come back!" *The Happening* is one of the worst films ever, and we've now watched it so many times we can practically recite it.

"If he can't appreciate *The Happening*, he's not the boy for you," Dad says. I actually agree a little bit, so *The Happening* it is.

Dan arrives with flowers for my mum and a bottle of wine for my dad. He finds the film as hilariously bad as we do and, afterwards, joins in the film and food matching game with impressive suggestions like *Hannibal* with steak tartare.

"How did I do?" he asks me as we're saying goodbye on the front step.

"Very well," I say, smiling. "Your impression of Mark Wahlberg was inspired."

He does it again – frowning so hard his eyes almost cross.

I laugh. And then I say, "They like you. I could tell."

"I like them," he says. "But not as much as I like you."

"I should think not," I say. And I realise that I hadn't worried about what he'd think of my mum. I hadn't even thought about it. For as long as I can remember, I've been comparing myself with either Jamie or Mum – and always assuming that people would be less impressed with me – and now I seemed to have stopped doing it, without even noticing.

Dan kisses me and I squirm a little bit, worrying about the neighbours seeing. We live on a small close, so we don't have many neighbours, but most of them are extremely nosey.

"No one's looking," Dan says. I smile as he kisses me again. Then he sets off down the path doing an exaggerated tiptoe and looking from side to side.

"Give over," I say, laughing. I follow him to the road, kiss him again and then he goes.

I'm smiling as I walk back up the drive. I spot something out of the corner of my eye: a piece of paper, flapping under the windscreen wiper of my mum's Audi. This happens quite a lot – adverts usually, the occasional political rant – and it's one thing that everyone on the Close agrees on: it drives them mad. I pull the paper out from under the wiper. It's folded in half and I almost stick it in my pocket without unfolding it, but then I do, and I feel myself go hot and then cold.

It was another page from my diary. Not an original page, a photocopy. Actually, two pages. Facing pages copied onto one piece of paper. It was stuff I'd written about Mum and Dad after they'd had a row a while ago. It wasn't as humiliating as the previous things, but I'd written it in the heat of the moment and I'd been upset. I'd said they were more interested in each other than in me and Jamie, and that they needed to grow up and start acting like responsible parents. I'd regretted it and, a few days later, I'd thought about tearing the pages out and throwing them away. But instead I'd stuck them together with Pritt Stick. But obviously not well enough. I'm so relieved I found it on the car before my parents did. I would have hated them to read it.

I show the pages to Dan when he comes to meet me at the deli for lunch. He doesn't read the whole thing, just scans it, but his face goes red and he looks furious and says, "Who is doing this?" I don't think he's expecting me to answer. He's just sounds frustrated.

I shake my head. "It could be anyone. Anyone who was at Jamie's party. But I've been thinking about it and I only just realised that it's been different each time. The first time – on Facebook – was for me. Then Maddy got the page in her pocket, then you got the text, and now this one was obviously for my parents' benefit."

"Which is why the stuff in the diary was about your parents."

I nod.

"So now I'm wondering who's next," I say.

"I don't know, but I think you should call the police," he says. "They've been to your house, Della."

"I know," I say, but I feel sick at the thought of it. Showing the police the messages I've had so far. Them reading the pages from my diary. They'd all be laughing at me behind my back. As if this isn't humiliating enough.

"No," I say. "I'm not doing that. It's going to stop sooner or later. Whoever's doing it will get bored."

"OK. But promise me that if there's any more, you'll at least tell your parents."

"I will," I tell him. I probably will.

Later that afternoon it's incredibly quiet in the deli – probably because it's so hot outside; everyone's out enjoying the sun rather than shopping for proscuitto or sundried tomatoes. In fact, the only customers we've had all day have been buying stuff for picnics – and so we decide to shut early. Mum's phoned and asked me to bring some food home, so I put together a selection of deli stuff: olives, mozzarella, potato salad, salami, and head home.

I haven't been able to stop thinking about my diary all day. There's no way I'm going to tell my parents – not yet, not until I absolutely have to – but I've also been thinking about what might happen next. I don't know what kind of reaction whoever's doing it is looking for. Presumably they can't see me when I get the messages or whatever, so what are they getting out of it? What are they hoping to achieve? And what's going to make them feel like they've done enough? And like Dan said, now they've been to my house. I hate to think they might have been watching me and waiting for the right moment.

When I get home, I check the car and look around to make sure there's nothing anywhere else. I feel sick thinking about it. The worst part is waiting for the next thing, which could happen at any time. It's horrible. And I hate keeping it from Mum and Dad too, but what could they do about it?

I let myself in and go straight through to say hello to my parents, who are sunbathing in the garden again. I set the salad and deli stuff out on the patio table, while Dad gets a bottle of Zinfandel and three glasses. I'm just buttering some French bread when the phone rings and I hear mum answer the cordless in the garden. I know immediately, just from the tone of her voice, that something's wrong.

And then I hear her almost shouting, "Is she OK? Is she OK?" and Dad runs past me out into the garden.

I drop the knife on the countertop and just stand there. I don't know what to do. I know it's a cliché to say that my legs turned to jelly, but I literally feel like if I try to walk, I'll just fall down.

I can hear Mum crying and Dad, who must have taken the phone, asking what happened, and when, and where, and how is she... But I can't even turn around. It's almost like if I move it'll make it more real. It's such a strange feeling.

And then Mum and Dad are in the kitchen and Mum puts her arms around me and says, "Your sister's been in an accident. She's OK. She's just got cuts and bruises, but..." and then she starts crying again. I manage to turn around and wrap my arms around her waist and my face is against her shoulder and I realise, because I feel her top getting wet, that I'm crying too.

"She's OK," Dad repeats, wrapping his arms around both of us. "She's OK."

After a few minutes, we manage to sit down at the dining table.

"What happened?" I ask.

Mum tears off a few sheets of kitchen roll and wipes her face.

"They're not exactly sure," Dad says. "It sounds like a few of them had gone off in a car to a party or a bar or something and then, on the way back, they ran off the road. Most of them are OK, but..."

Mum starts crying again.

"What?" I say. My hands are shaking so much that I move them under my legs and sit on them.

"The driver died," Dad says simply.

Within a couple of hours, I'm home alone. Mum and Dad have gone to California. They weren't sure at first about leaving me, but I talked them into it. I could have gone with them – although they weren't sure about that either, I think they wanted to protect me – but I didn't want to. Yes, I'm worried about Jamie, of course, but... I don't know. I think I was scared.

Mum and Dad made me ring Maddy before they

left, and she should be here any minute. I also rang Dan and he's coming too. I wasn't sure about asking him. I didn't want it to look like as soon as my parents went away to take care of my injured and, presumably, traumatised sister, I invited my boyfriend over. But I really wanted him here, so I decided not to worry about how it would look to anyone but me. It's not as if he's going to stay the night.

Me, Maddy and Dan are all sitting in the lounge. We've put a DVD on – *Green Wing* – but none of us is really watching it.

"So was the driver drunk?" Maddy asks. She's sitting on the beanbag in the corner of the room.

"I don't know," I say. "I can't imagine he would be. They'd driven to the party so he must've been the – what do they call it? – designated driver." I'm leaning back against Dan who's sitting in the corner of the sofa.

I always thought I'd be embarrassed to be like this with Dan: in my house, in front of Maddy. But I'm not. It feels right, despite the circumstances. I'm glad that Dan's here. He makes me feel safe.

"Just because he was meant to be the designated driver doesn't mean he didn't drink," Dan says.

"I don't know," I say. "It's horrible, whatever happened."

"I know," Maddy says, "I keep thinking how scary it would be to be in an accident like that in a foreign country, far away from your family. I mean, anything like that happens, you're going to want your mum, aren't you?"

"Did you not want to go, too?" Dan asks me.

I shake my head slowly. "No. I don't know why." I glance at the TV and see Dr Todd using a car air freshener as deodorant. "I was scared, I suppose."

"What of?" Maddy asks.

I sigh. "Me and Jamie aren't that close..."

"Yeah, but—" Maddy starts to say.

"No, I just felt like it was too much. Too much for me to deal with. Does that sound terrible?"

"No," Maddy says. "I know what you mean. I was the same when my gran died. I knew she was dying, but I couldn't go and see her and confirm it."

"Did you see her before she died?" Dan asks.

Maddy shakes her head. "I just couldn't do it. I regret it, but I couldn't do it."

"That's OK, though," Dan says. "If that's how you felt, that's OK."

"Dan's mum's a psychologist," I say, smiling. "He's all about honouring your feelings."

"No, I agree," Maddy says. "I beat myself up about it, but I also think, well, that's how I felt and who's to say I was wrong? I couldn't deal with it, why should I force myself? If I'd been older when it happened then maybe, but I wasn't and that's OK. I'm sure my gran would've understood. In fact, I don't think she would have wanted me to see her like that anyway."

"Well, I mean, things aren't that bad with Jamie, obviously," I say. "I think part of it is that I've felt so much better while she's been away..."

"Yeah, she does overshadow you a bit," Maddy says.

"What do you mean?" I ask.

"Well, she's always been the bossy one, the one who demands all the attention. From your parents, from your friends, even. You know, even when we were quite little, I'd come round to play. Me and you would be playing quite happily and then Jamie would come and kick off, pick a fight, nick something of yours or something. And then you and Jamie would be fighting and your mum would have to come and deal with it and then everything was all about Jamie."

"I don't remember that," I say. It's strange. I know that Maddy's telling the truth, but if I'd actually thought about what happened, I would think that Jamie and Maddy wanted to play and I was spoiling their fun. I always felt like a spare part growing up. Shit.

"I just thought of something," I say. I tell them and then say, "Maybe that's why I didn't want to go. I didn't want to feel like a spare part in the big family drama. It was better to stay out of it than to feel like I didn't belong." I start to cry. "Shit."

Dan squeezes me and kisses the top of my head. "You shouldn't feel guilty about it. It's not your fault."

"But—" is as far as I get before Maddy interrupts: "It's your family's fault if you feel that way.

I have to say, though, it's never the impression I've got. You've always seemed like a lovely family to me. I've always been envious of your relationship with your parents." She laughs. "Not so much with Jamie though."

I lean back so that my face is against Dan's neck and I inhale. I actually feel more comfortable now, with him, than I would sitting here with my sister. Of course, I wouldn't be sniffing my sister's neck.

"All the others are OK, right?" Maddy says. "The others in the accident?"

I wonder if she's changing the subject back to the accident because she's not comfortable with me and Dan being so cosy. But I've been the gooseberry with her and Sid loads of times over the years. Once, I stayed the night at Maddy's, and her mum and stepdad went out. She snuck Sid in and – and I'm not kidding – they were well on the way to actually having sex in Maddy's bed, while I tried to sleep on a blow-up bed on the floor. I spent probably ten or fifteen minutes listening to them sighing and slurping and giggling before I freaked out and yelled at them and they remembered I was there and knocked it on the head. It still makes me hot with embarrassment to think about it.

"I think they're mostly OK, yeah," I say. Dan takes my hand and strokes my fingers. "Some of them have worse injuries than Jamie, but there's definitely nothing life-threatening."

"But the driver died..." Maddy says and we all just sit there for a little while. I can't get my head around the idea that my sister was in a car with someone who died. I wonder if they knew he was dead. I wonder how it happened. Whether they all knew it was going to happen. I can't imagine how scary that would be – to be driving along, on the way back from a party, laughing, joking, singing, whatever – and to suddenly realise you were about to crash and would likely be hurt or even killed. It must have been terrifying.

I wonder if that's another reason I didn't want to go. The idea of it scares me too much.

"I'm just going to pop to the loo," Maddy says. I was right, I think. She's giving me and Dan a bit of time alone together and she was right to go since, as soon as she leaves the room, Dan kisses me. I'm just sort of melting into it (it really feels like I'm melting; I can't feel the sofa underneath me any more) when Dan pulls back and says, "Is this OK?"

"What?" I say. I feel dizzy.

"Kissing you. I don't want you to feel like, you know, your sister's in hospital and I'm all, you know..."

I smile. "All over me?"

He grins. "Yeah."

"No, it's fine," I say. "I like it. It takes my mind off...everything."

21

In the morning, I'm woken by the phone ringing. It's my parents to tell me that everything's fine with Jamie. She's got cuts and bruises and a sprained wrist. There were six of them in the car, which was actually a pick-up truck. Four of them were sitting in the back, including Jamie and they were actually thrown out of the truck, which they think is why they weren't as badly hurt as they might have been. The front seat passenger has got broken arms and quite bad facial injuries.

"And the driver?" I ask.

"Sweetie, he died," Mum says.

"I know. I just meant... Do they know more about why?"

"He wasn't wearing his seatbelt. And they think he'd been drinking."

"Did Jamie know him well?"

There's a bit of a silence and then Mum says, "I think so. She hasn't really talked about it very much."

"What was his name?" I ask. I don't know why, but I do.

"Nathan," she says.

She tells me that Jamie seems very disturbed by it all, but the doctors have told them that's normal and they just have to wait until she feels like talking about it. She says that she and Dad are fine and then says, "Are you OK, sweetheart?"

"I'm fine," I say. "Maddy stayed."

"Oh good. I'm glad you weren't on your own."

"So give Dad a kiss for me. And give Jamie my love."

"I will. Be careful. Take care of yourself and don't worry about us. Everything's fine."

I hang up the phone and go straight to the computer. "Sorry," I say to Maddy, who's stretching and groaning. "I just need to check something."

I bring up my Googlemail and search for the original email from Jamie.

"Look at this," I say to Maddy. She clambers out of bed and stands next to me in her *High School Musical* pyjamas that she claims are ironic (but I'm not so sure).

I read her the bit about Nathan and then tell her that it was him who died.

"Shit," Maddy says.

"Should I tell Mum and Dad?" I ask. "I mean, they said that Jamie isn't talking about it or anything and maybe she's upset because he was her boyfriend or something."

"Yeah, but she'd be upset anyway, surely. Even if he was just a friend. Jesus, even if you didn't know him, you'd still be upset."

"No, I know. But maybe it could help. If he was her boyfriend, I mean. Maybe it could help them help her, if they knew."

"I don't know," Maddy says, getting back into bed. "Do you think maybe you're just trying to get involved?"

"No... I don't think so."

"I don't mean in a bad way. I just mean that maybe you want to do something to help. You know, 'cos you're feeling powerless or something."

I turn the computer off. "I don't know. I just think maybe I should mention it."

"Well, do then. I mean, go with what you feel. If you think it's important, it's better to say it and be wrong than not to say anything."

"And be wrong," I say. "That's what I was thinking."

Dan meets me from work. He's got a Tesco's bag with him and, when I ask what's in it, he says, "I thought I'd cook you dinner."

"Really?" I say. "At my house?"

"Yeah. Is that OK?"

"Of course. No one's ever cooked for me before. Except my parents."

"Well I make a great spaghetti bolognaise, even if I do say so myself."

When we get home, Dan gets on with cooking dinner and I ring Mum at their hotel. I tell her what Jamie's email said about Nathan and then I say,

"Was I right to tell you?"

"Of course," she says. "Jamie hasn't really even said whether she knows him – I mean, knew him – at all. I'll mention this to the doctors and see if they think we should bring it up with her. It's hard to know what to do for the best."

I hear her voice crack and I know that she's crying. And then Dad comes on the phone: "Hey, my little chickadee," he says.

"I'm sorry I upset Mum," I say.

"Oh no, don't say that!" he says. "It's just hard, you know. Being in another country. We don't really know what's going on. Jamie's not herself. She's bound to be traumatised and it's hard for me and your mum to see. And she's missing you."

"Jamie?" I say, startled.

"Well, yes. Of course," he says. "But I meant your mum."

I actually blush. How mad is that? I blush because I thought for a minute that my sister might be missing me.

"And we're not really sleeping," he says. "Jetlag. And you know what it's like when you go to sleep – you start thinking of what could have happened."

"Yeah," I say. I know. I did the same thing last night. I felt knackered until I got into bed and then lay there thinking that it could have been Jamie that had been killed. I was surprised at how that made me feel. It was like being punched in the stomach. I ended up clutching one of my pillows and it took me ages to fall asleep.

By the time I've finished talking to my dad, Dan's got everything simmering away. He sits down at the dining table and I take my place opposite him.

"How are they getting on?" he asks.

I tell him about the email and give him a rundown of the conversation we've just had.

"She'll probably need counselling when she gets back," he says.

I smile. "Stop pimping for your mum."

He pulls a horrified face. "That's a mental image I could do without. But they'll probably refer her on the NHS. They're really hot on that kind of thing now. And she should do it."

I feel suddenly exhausted and my eyes fill with tears. Dan stands up, walks around the table and wraps his arms around me from behind.

"I don't want to talk about it any more," I say. "Is that really selfish? And don't tell me to accept my feelings." I laugh.

"Very selfish," he says, kissing the back of my neck. "But that's OK. You hungry?"

Literally the minute he asks me that, my stomach rumbles loudly.

"Wow," he says, laughing. "You're really suggestible."

I watch him as he dishes out the spaghetti bolognese and salad and takes garlic bread out of the oven. While we eat, we talk about pretty much everything but Jamie's situation. We talk about school, people we like, people we don't. Teachers, subjects. He tells me more about graphic design and what he wants to do when he leaves school. After clearing away the dishes, he produces two chocolate mousses out of the fridge.

"Where did they come from?" I ask.

"I brought them."

"Wow. You're amazing."

I get up from the table and slide my arms around his waist. Grinning, he puts the mousses back in the fridge. "We can eat them later," he says.

"Yep," I say.

I grab his hand and pull him into the lounge and down on the sofa. We're kissing before we even land on the seat and I end up on top of him. And it's amazing. I've never lain on top of a boy before and it feels...incredible.

We're kissing and his hand slides up the back of my shirt. My first feeling is to pull away, but I tell myself to just go with it. (No, I really do. I hear myself think, "Just go with it.") Instead of pulling away, I roll towards the back of the sofa, which means I can slide my hand up the front of his T-shirt. His stomach is warm, which I was kind of expecting or at least I would have been, had I even thought for a minute that I'd be putting my hand inside Dan's clothes this evening. (Which, obviously, I kind of did, although I didn't admit it to myself.) But it's also – Dan's stomach, I mean – a little bit hairy and I hadn't been expecting that at all. It seems so...grown up.

I know how that sounds. I know that I'm lying on the sofa with a boy's hand on my back and my hand up his T-shirt, but still. It surprises me. And then I have a moment of worry about whether there is actually any hair on my belly, but I realise it's way too late to do anything about that now and so I just carry on.

"You are so gorgeous," he whispers. I literally can't believe it. I can't believe I'm lying here, half on top of Dan Bailey, whose hand is creeping up towards my bra – is he planning on undoing it, I wonder? – and he's just told me I'm gorgeous. Gorgeous!

Dan's hand slides away from my bra strap. OK then, so he's not going to undo my bra. But then it slides under the front of my top, across my stomach. I automatically suck it in and then I'm annoyed with myself. He's just said I'm gorgeous. I know my stomach's not fat and, even if it was, he thinks I'm gorgeous.

I kiss him deeper, leaning up on my elbow to get more comfortable. Honestly, I feel like I could lie here kissing him all night. In fact, maybe I could.

I'm home alone. I suddenly picture that kid, Kevin, from the film *Home Alone* and I laugh.

"What?" Dan says, against my mouth.

I laugh and pull back a little. "I'm sorry. I was just thinking about that film, *Home Alone*."

He frowns. "Right. You know there's a time and a place..."

I laugh again. "No. I was thinking that I was home alone and then it made me think of the film."

"You're not home alone. I'm here with you."

"Yeah, but I was thinking that we could do this all night because my parents aren't coming home."

"All night, eh?" he says, smiling.

I suddenly feel a bit self-conscious. We've still got our hands under each other's clothes, after all.

"Well, maybe not all night..." I say.

"I could do this all night," he says, and starts kissing me again.

His hand slides higher and I move my hand higher too, but then I touch his nipple and, without even thinking of it, I yank my hand back down. Nipple. I wasn't expecting that. I mean, I know boys have nipples, I just...wasn't expecting to touch one.

And...oh. Dan's hand has moved higher too and he's touching my nipple. He doesn't seem to have been quite as surprised to find it as I was to find his. He's stroking it through my bra and I've never felt anything like it in my life. I mean, I've touched it myself, of course, but this is completely different. I feel like I'm seeing stars.

I roll on top of Dan, trapping his hand between us and it feels even better. We stay like that for a while and I don't know what's supposed to happen next. In fact, I don't think I want anything else to happen. I'm not sure I'm ready for anything else. Yet.

The next day, Maddy comes to meet me for lunch and, because it's a lovely day again, we take our lunch to the park and stretch out on the freshly mown grass.

I tell her about last night with Dan and she grins. "It's going well!"

I laugh. "It is."

"And what did you think?"

"About...?"

"You know. About the kissing and the touching and the nipple twiddling..."

I see a man sitting on a nearby bench stop reading his *Daily Express* and I smile. "It was great."

"Better than you thought?"

"Yeah."

"So will you be...?" She raises her eyebrows.

I glance at *Express*-guy. He's quite clearly listening. I think about packing our stuff up and going and sitting somewhere and then I think: why do I care what he thinks of me? I don't know him.

"I should think so," I say.

Maddy just smiles and doesn't say anything else, which is very unlike her.

"What?" I ask.

"What?" she says.

"You look like you've got something to say..."

She shakes her head.

"Maddy!" I say, glancing at the *Express*-guy again. I might not care what he thinks of me, but I'm interested to know he's still listening.

"Is it about you and Leo?" I ask.

"Kind of," she says. "I talked to Sid."

"Oh my God. What did he say?"

Her face falls for a second and she takes a swig of her Diet Coke. "Well, at first he was really upset, understandably."

I nod.

"But then I told him that I didn't actually want to break up and he got a bit freaked out."

"Why?"

"Because of Leo."

"But what did you say about Leo?"

"I told him that I wanted to sleep with him. Basically."

Express-guy actually turns to look at us. I feel the urge to tell him where to get off, but I don't. He's probably getting off on the conversation as it is.

"So what did he say?" I ask.

"We had a really good talk, actually," she says. "I mean, we talked about all the things we haven't been talking about. All the things we've avoided talking about. About sex. And Leo."

"And?"

She sighs. "He said I should sleep with him."

"With who?"

"With Leo."

"What?"

Express-guy has given up all pretence of not listening to us and has now half-turned towards us.

"He said he doesn't want to lose me and if I feel like I need to sleep with Leo then I should."

"Was he pissed?"

She laughs. "No. I asked him that."

"So what did you say?"

"Well I didn't really say anything. I was too shocked."

"So what's he suggesting? Like an open relationship?"

"Yeah, I think so."

She glances up at *Express*-guy – who I didn't realise she'd even noticed – and says, "Will you stop earwigging our fucking conversation."

He gets up and practically scurries away.

"Are you OK?" I ask Maddy because, really, that was out of character.

"No, I'm freaked out. I'd kind of resigned myself to the idea of splitting up with Sid and being with Leo. So then for Sid to say, yeah, that's fine, go ahead. I don't know what to do."

"What do you want to do?"

"I honestly don't know. Can you love two boys at once, do you think?"

"You can love an infinite number of people, so I don't see why you shouldn't be able to love two boys. I mean, you already loved Leo as a friend, didn't you?"

She nods. "It just seems so...strange. I've never heard of it before."

"You've heard of an open relationship."

"Yeah, but not at our age. I always think an open relationship is like old hippies, or swingers, or something."

"Well, yeah, but it goes on at our age, too. But everyone doesn't know about it."

"What do you mean?"

"Like it would be normal for you to just start sleeping with Leo behind Sid's back. It's only Sid saying it's OK that makes it weird."

"I suppose. But it is still weird."

"Yeah."

Dan meets me after work again. It's become a routine and I really love it. We walk back to mine holding hands. It's still gorgeous – the sun is shining, but it's not so stiflingly warm any more. In fact, it's the perfect weather, so we walk through the park. It's really busy and there's even a bunch of people playing frisbee. I feel like we're in America or something. In fact, I feel like I'm in a film. As we walk, I see it playing in my head: Me and Dan at the cinema, cuddling up on my sofa, Dan cooking for me, sitting on the bench at the party... I need a song to be playing over the top of it. I'm trying to think of one, when Dan says, "What are you thinking about?"

"I was thinking that I feel like I'm in a film. And what song could be playing over the top."

He laughs. "Right. Er."

I laugh. "You actually don't need to think of one."

"But I want to now. 'Chico Time'?"

"Er. No."

"'I Like to Move it, Move it'?"

"OK. That's plenty."

"That Cheeky Girls song?"

"That's more than enough."

He pulls my hand so my arm is around his waist and he drops his arm around my shoulders. "I'll try and think of something more romantic."

"If you would," I say.

We get to the river and stop to have a look at the ducks. He turns and kisses me and then asks, "When are you expecting your parents back?"

Leaning my elbow on the railing, I turn to look at him. I think I know why he's asking. In fact, I'm sure I know. "Another couple of days, I think."

"Right."

"So..." I take a deep breath and I can already feel myself starting to blush, but I say it anyway. "Do you want to stay the night? It doesn't have to be tonight, but..."

"I can stay tonight," he says.

"Really?"

"Yeah." He stares at me. "Is that OK?"

My stomach is flipping over and over and I'm not convinced I can speak so I just nod. Dan leans forward and kisses me and I suddenly feel like I can't get home quick enough. It's only about five minutes through the park and then another five to my house. My hand is shaking so much I can barely open the door, but then I feel Dan's hands on my waist and I start to relax. I don't have to do anything

I don't want to. I know he's not going to push me. We go inside and I'm worried for a second that we'll be going straight upstairs, but we don't. We walk into the lounge and sit down on the sofa.

"So what do you think?" he says. "DVD and a takeaway?"

I must admit, I feel relieved. This is such a weird situation. We both know exactly what's going to happen (well...not exactly, but close enough), but we don't really know when or how. It's so unnatural.

We debate what DVD to watch for a while, but finally settle on *Spinal Tap*, another of my favourites – it's my dad's favourite film of all time – that Dan has never seen. We phone for Chinese food and settle down on the sofa. We eat the food, watch the film, cuddle up and then, fairly soon (it's a pretty short film), we're both just sitting there.

And we know what's next. But how?

"So this is a bit weird, isn't it?" Dan says.

I laugh. "I know. I don't understand how you, you know, get from one state of affairs to the other state of affairs."

"You mean, 'How did the war start?'" Dan says

and I laugh. I'm glad he can quote *Blackadder* too.
Since he'd never seen either *Gregory's Girl* or *Spinal
Tap*, I was starting to worry. I'm glad he knows his
classic comedy.

"Yeah," I say. "Or how do we get from the sofa to
the bedroom."

Dan stands up and reaches his hand out to me.
I take his hand and follow him as he leads me up to
my own bedroom. It feels even weirder when we get
there. I mean, this is my room. My own space. The
things I've done in here. It's so strange to have a boy
in here. Again. I mean, it was weird enough when
Dan came in during the party, but now? It doesn't
entirely feel right. I know that Maddy lost her
virginity in her parents' bed, but that would feel
even worse, I think.

We sit down on the bed and part of me just wants
to get it out of the way, so that it's done and I don't
need to worry about it any more. But another part of
me wants to kind of savour it. I mean, this is never
going to happen again. It's something in your life
that only ever happens once. I want to remember it.
I want it to be perfect (although I know, since

enough of my friends have told me, that it's likely to be disappointing).

Dan says, "You've never done this before?"

I laugh. "No. How could you tell?"

He smiles at me. "Don't worry about it. We don't have to do anything you don't want to do. Just keep talking." He laughs and then adds: "I don't mean the whole time."

So...we did it. And it was...good. Really good. But weird. I kept saying, "This is so weird" until I'd said it so many times I thought I heard Dan sigh and so then I had to force myself to stop saying it, but I still wanted to burble out.

It just seemed like such a strange thing to be doing. I mean, if you think about sex, it's kind of odd, isn't it? But it was nice. I'm glad that it was Dan. He made it all really easy and almost-natural – even the condom bit, which could have heen hideous – but I'm sure the first time never feels entirely natural, does it?

Afterwards was better. We were lying in my bed, which was still weird, but we were just talking and kissing and he'd put his boxers back on and I put a T-shirt on and it was like it was before.

I wasn't really sure if I wanted Dan to stay because I really wanted to talk to Maddy about it, to tell her what had happened and ask her certain questions. I think I thought talking about it would make it seem more real or help me get it clear in my head, but Dan said he could stay and he did and I was glad. We didn't really sleep much, we talked most of the night and that was amazing. We talked about everything: our childhoods, our families, hopes and dreams and fears and all that stuff. It was easy because it was dark and I found myself telling him all sorts of things, things I never thought I'd tell anyone, and it was fine. He held my hands and played with my fingers and kissed my neck and stroked my hair and it was lovely. Still weird, but lovely.

23

I feel a bit embarrassed when I first wake up. I've never woken up with a boy before and I'm worried about my hair and whether I've got mascara all round my eyes and – ugh! – morning breath. But when Dan rolls over and smiles at me, I feel OK again. Tired since I don't think we fell asleep until about four in the morning, but happy that he's here. And a little bit worried that he'll want to do it again, which I'm not sure I'm up for, particularly not now because it's light. However, he doesn't make any moves and we just kiss and talk until I can't put it off any longer; I have to get up and get ready for work.

Once we're dressed and downstairs, sitting at the table and having breakfast I start finding it all weird again.

"What?" Dan asks, spreading Marmite too thickly on his toast.

"It's just weird," I say.

He smiles. "Yeah, you mentioned that last night. Once or twice."

"I know. I'm sorry. But look at us. It's like we're playing house! It's—"

"Weird, yeah. I know what you mean. I've never done this before either."

My mouth must drop open because he laughs and says, "This, not that. I've done that before, but I've never stayed the night and done the breakfast thing."

"Right," I say. I want to ask him how many times he has done that and who with, but I think that might be easier to talk about in the dark.

We finish breakfast, get all our stuff together and then set off out – me to work, Dan home. He tells me he's going to sleep until it's time to meet me from work.

*

Dan is waiting for me when I come out of the deli. As soon as I see him, sitting on the low wall, his face turned up to the sun, I want to kiss him. So I do. We walk home through the park, but as we approach my house I start to feel nervous. I've actually got butterflies and, as I put the key in the door, my hand is shaking a bit.

Although walking through the park was just the same, things have changed between us. I mean, once you start doing it, you don't stop, do you? You don't just do it the once. Once you've done it the once, you then do it pretty much every time you're together. Or whenever you can, anyway. At least, I think so. I don't doubt that Dan's expecting us to go to bed again tonight.

I'm not sure what to do, so I think I might as well just repeat last night as well as I can. So I phone for a takeaway and we put the TV on. *Dude, Where's My Car?* is on Film4 and since that's one of my guilty pleasures, we watch that.

Well, it's on, anyway. We spend most of the time kissing.

We're interrupted by the phone. Again. And it's my mum and dad again. They say Jamie's feeling a bit better and the three of them are coming home at the weekend.

After I hang up the phone, Dan's looking at me a bit funny. At first I think it's because he wants to turn the film off and head upstairs, but then he says, "I've just thought of something."

"What?"

"You're not going to like it."

"What?"

"It's just a thought. It might be complete bollocks."

"You're freaking me out! What?"

"Well, when did your diary go missing?"

"You know. The night of my party."

"Did it? Or was that the last time you saw it?"

"What do you mean?"

"I mean, you assumed it went missing that night, but when did you actually notice it had gone?"

"The next morning."

"Right. And then you started to get the messages?"

"Yeah."

"And the last one was the night I came to dinner?"

"Yeah." I have no idea what he's getting at, honestly.

"Well I was just thinking that your diary went missing when your sister went to California and the messages stopped when she had her accident."

24

Mum and Dad ring to tell me that they've landed. I feel quite sick because I still haven't decided what to say to Jamie. I feel quite sure that Dan is right, but then I was sure it was Gemima Lee and I was wrong about that. I don't want to accuse my sister and then find that it wasn't her at all. I mean, we've never been that close, but accusing her of something like that would be likely to permanently damage our relationship, wouldn't it?

It will take them about an hour to get home from the airport, so I decide to have a bath and think about it. I've always done my best thinking in the bath. I run it hot with loads of bubbles and then just lie back. I've got an awful lot to think about.

Everything's changed since Jamie's party. A lot of it for the better. Dan insists that he would have asked me out at some point, but I don't know. It seems to me that if it hadn't happened at the party, it wouldn't have happened at all. And I can't believe how glad I am that it did. I mean, I'd liked Dan for years and fantasised about what it would be like to go out with him (and more), but it's actually better than I imagined. He's so incredibly lovely. It still amazes me that he's friends with a cow like Gemima Lee, but I don't need to concern myself with that.

The best thing that's come of all of this is that I know myself a lot better. I'm a lot more confident. I care less about what people think. That's partly thanks to Dan, but it's partly my own work too. And, like Maddy says, it's partly because Jamie's been away. I was never really aware of it, but I have been in her shadow and I have let her overshadow me. She's always made everything about her, and I've always let her.

Which makes sense that she would have been pissed off if she saw Jack kiss me. She would have hated for Jack to be kissing me at her party. On her big night. After she'd broken up with him and was going off for her big, life-changing summer abroad.

And it would have been easy for her to harass me from California. She had her laptop and anything else she could have got Danielle to do. I thought Danielle was a bit weird at Cobby's party, but I assumed it was because she was with Jack. But Maddy found the diary page in her pocket the day after the party, so Danielle could easily have slipped it in there. And Danielle knows where we live, of course – she's been here loads of times with Jamie.

It all makes sense. I think.

I slide lower in the water and drop my head back. It feels lovely. Almost too hot, but not quite. Or too hot in a good way. But what will I say to Jamie? Dan suggested that I just tell her – and Mum and Dad at the same time – exactly what's been happening and wait for her to own up. The only trouble with that plan is that, if it wasn't Jamie, she'll piss herself laughing. But I'm not supposed to care about that, am I? And I don't. But I do. God. I'm not getting anywhere. I'm just going round in circles.

I get out of the bath, dry off, get dressed and go downstairs. I make myself a drink and sit at the kitchen table. The back door's open because it's really hot again, so I hear my family before I see them. I hear the car pull into the drive and the doors opening and closing. I hear Dad making some feeble joke and Mum laughing (she always laughs at his feeble jokes). I can't hear Jamie, but I know she's with them. Where else would she be?

The front door opens and I actually feel like I'm going to be sick. I seem to have spent a lot of this summer feeling sick, between everything. And yet, it's got to be done.

The three of them come in and I stand up and hug Mum. She squeezes me tight and kisses me on the temple. I know I enjoyed myself while they were away, but I hadn't realised how much I'd missed them until just now. Dad picks me up and swings me round. But only a little. He's been doing that since I was small, but he can't manage it quite as well any more. He rubs his stubble on my face, like he's also been doing since I was small.

"Is Dan here?" Dad asks, pretending to look under the table and heading as if to open the cupboard under the stairs.

"Oh, shut up," I say, smiling.

I step towards Jamie who looks...odd. She looks like herself, but not quite. Like she's a zombie version of Jamie. Or an *Invasion of the Bodysnatchers* version. She kind of looks spaced out. Maybe they had to drug her to get her on the plane. Before I even get close to her, she turns and walks out of the room. Me, Mum and Dad all just stand there, listening to her footsteps going up the stairs.

"She doesn't look...right," I say and Mum sighs and rubs her face.

"No, she's not. She's still on tranquilisers and she's just... Well, the doctor thinks she's suffering from Post Traumatic Stress Disorder."

Dad puts the kettle on and me and Mum sit down at the kitchen table. "Is everything OK with you?" Mum asks me.

"Sort of," I say. "Everything's great with Dan, but

something's been happening over the summer and I need to talk to you about it."

"Oh, God," Dad says, turning back from sorting the cups and teabags and everything. "We're not going to have a sex talk, are we? Can't you look it up on the internet?"

Mum laughs, but I shake my head. "No, it's not about that. Listen."

And I tell them about the diary. About it going missing. About the Facebook message. And the page put in Maddy's pocket. The text message to Dan. And the photocopy on the car.

They sit there in silence the entire time, although I can see from their faces that they're kind of horrified by it.

"So what do you think?" I ask.

"What do you mean?" Mum asks.

"Are you embarrassed? Ashamed?"

"God, no!" Mum says and Dad stands up and comes around to hug me. "I feel awful that this has happened to you," he says. "What a horrible thing to go through."

"It sort of was..." I start to say.

"Sort of?" Mum says. "When I was your age, it would have been my worst nightmare!"

"Yeah, but you probably had much more exciting stuff in your diary than there was in mine," I say, smiling. "But, listen, that's not all."

And then I tell them Dan's theory about Jamie.

Epilogue

Jamie's having counselling. In fact, we're all having counselling. Family counselling. Great. Dan's pleased though. No, it's not with his mum, but he's been proved right. Smart arse. Even the sweetest boy likes to be proved right.

As soon as Mum and Dad confronted Jamie, she admitted to it. She wasn't shocked. She didn't deny it. She didn't even seem to care or think it was that big a deal. And it was exactly as we thought: she saw me kissing Jack (it was Jack kissing me, but whatever) and then, the next day, saw my diary and took it. She was just planning on reading it at first. I think she thought maybe there had been something going on with me and him and she wanted to know, but then she just decided to try and humiliate me.

The thing that surprised, I think, all of us the most is that she was a virgin when she went to America. That's what she was referring to in her email to Danielle (the one she sent to me), about Nathan being the one. And he was. Sort of. She did lose her virginity to him and it sounds as if she had a massive crush on him (if not more) and then he died. And the accident was his fault. Because he was drunk.

Maddy is planning on breaking up with Sid. Although she liked to pretend it was cool, sleeping with both of them, it was really messing with her head and she's finally admitted that it's over with Sid and she's in love with Leo. It's such a shame because it was always the three of them and now it's presumably going to ruin Leo's friendship with

Sid (how could it not?), but they're going to give it a go and see how they get on.

And me and Dan are fine. Better than fine, in fact. Dan saw some graffiti the other day and rang me to tell me about it. It said, "Good girls keep diaries. Bad girls don't have time." I guess it's true. I used to worry about being a good girl. I thought it meant I was dull and boring. But now I realise it just means I'm good. And it doesn't even mean I'll always be good. I can be anything I want to be. Things change. People change. Opportunities come along. Your own flesh and blood can turn against you out of spite. The boy you thought would never look at you can fall in love with you. (And he is in love with me, he's told me. And I've told him I love him too.)

Everyone changes. Everything changes. And that's OK. In fact, it's better than OK. It's life.

Keris says:

I've been making up stories for as long as I can remember, but I didn't manage to write a novel until 2004 when I took part in National Novel Writing Month. I haven't quite finished that one yet, but I have finished a few others (Della Says: OMG! is the first to be published).

I love American TV, Russell Brand, Starbucks, New York, Jason Mraz, Take That, Twitter and pugs. And chocolate. One day, I'd like to travel around Europe in a camper van (with a satellite dish).

I co-founded the teen books blog Chicklish (www. chicklish.co.uk) and I blog about books at Five Minutes Peace (www.fiveminutespeace.co.uk). My website is www.keris-stainton.com and you can follow me at twitter.com/Keris.

I live in Lancashire with my husband and two young sons, who make me laugh every day (sometimes intentionally).

Send us **YOUR** diary confessions and win an iPod Touch!

Are you willing to share your secret confessions with the world?

Tell us your embarrassing story, or even take an extract from your diary – in 150 words or fewer.

Email your entry to

keris.says@googlemail.com

And we will feature it on **www.keris-stainton.com**. Blog visitors will then vote for the best entry, which will win the iPod Touch!

Of course your entry will be anonymous, as we wouldn't want what happened to Della to happen to you!

Closing date: 31st August 2010

Full terms and conditions available online